KT-152-940

22158392W

WITHDRAWN

27 JAN 2009

ERE'S AN O'FARRELL MOTHER

"I knew that warlock's
enough to last."

"It lasted for six generations," Phoebe told him.
"That's longer than you should've lasted."

"And your
Gortag
begin with

"She does," Juliana snapped. "We all do. And as
soon as we find hers, she and I are going to
destroy you just the way you deserve."

Paige was looking at Gortag's tail. The very end
flicked back and forth the way a cat's did when
it was hunting. *That's not good*, she thought.
What was he up to?

"I think we should just vanquish him now," she said
aloud. "We know he's not the one who took Lily's
powers. There's no reason to keep him around."

"I agree," Phoebe said. "We can use Juliana's
kitchen to make a potion."

But Gortag had begun to laugh. It was a deep
sound, almost a growl, that filled the entire
room. "You can't vanquish me!" he cackled.
"You don't even know where I am!"

More titles in the

Pocket Books series

All Pocket Books are available by post from:
Simon & Schuster Cash Sales. PO Box 29
Douglas, Isle of Man IM99 1BQ
Credit cards accepted.
Please telephone 01624 836000
fax 01624 670923
Internet http://www.bookpost.co.uk
or email: bookshop@enterprise.net for details

Charmed ™

INHERIT THE WITCH

An original novel by Laura J. Burns

Based on the hit TV series created by

Constance M. Burge

Pocket Books, London

22158392 W

CLACKMANNANSHIRE
LIBRARIES

WITHDRAWN

First published in Great Britain in 2004 by Pocket Books.
An imprint of Simon & Schuster UK Ltd.
Africa House, 64–78 Kingsway, London WC2B 6AH

Originally published in 2004 by Simon Spotlight,
an imprint of Simon & Schuster Children's Division, New York

™ & © 2004 by Spelling Television Inc. All Rights Reserved.

POCKET BOOKS and colophon are registered trademarks of Simon & Schuster.
A CIP catalogue record for this book is available from the British Library
upon request.

ISBN 0 7434 8958 6

3 5 7 9 10 8 6 4

Printed by Cox & Wyman Ltd, Reading, Berkshire

INHERIT THE
WITCH

Prologue

The witch sprinkled crushed rowan leaves onto the wooden floor, taking great care as she formed them into a magic circle. The spell had to work. It was her only hope.

The girl watched, eyes wide.

The circle was complete. The witch took a deep breath. It had been many years since she'd sought the company of her own kind, but the situation was dire. She knelt in the center of the magic circle and closed her eyes. She cleared her mind.

The girl was afraid. The witch had said that others were not to be trusted. She'd said that their location could never be revealed to anyone who understood that magic was real and true. Only the ignorant mortals could know of the witch and her daughter. Only among the mortals would they be safe.

The witch began to speak, imploring the goddess for help."Mother Earth, heed me. In this
hour of need, I seek solace. Send to me aid in my
trouble."

The witch's eyes flew open. She could feel the
magic working. In the air above her head floated
a picture, blurred, like a dream. A house. Tall
and imposing. Victorian. The witch memorized
the house, imprinting it on her psyche. The
magic whispered in her ear of other witches,
powerful witches. They were connected to this
house. They would help her. But could she trust
them?

The girl stared at the house in the air, dazzled
by the beauty of the magic. She wanted to rush
to that house, to live in it. There were witches
there, somehow she just knew it. But would they
be safe there, the witch and her daughter?

Would they be safe anywhere?

Chapter

1

"**Paige, can** you get the door?" Piper Halliwell yelled, quickly throwing on some clothes. The doorbell had already rung twice. "Paige?"

There was no answer from her half sister's room. Piper pulled a sweater over her head—hair still wet from the shower—as the doorbell rang again. "Coming!" she bellowed. It was no use. Halliwell Manor was a big house. No one standing outside would be able to hear her up on the second floor. "Where is everybody?" she muttered, yanking open her bedroom door. Usually everyone was slow to get going on Monday mornings. But today even her White-lighter husband, Leo, had been gone when she woke up. As she hurried toward the stairs, Paige's door opened.

"What's going on?" she asked sleepily. Her hair was a mess.

"There's someone at the door and they're not going away."

"What time is it?"

Piper glanced at the clock on the wall. "Seven thirty," she said. It *was* a little early for visitors. Paige just yawned and closed her door. With a sigh Piper headed down the stairs. She knew Paige wasn't a morning person. Their sister, Phoebe, on the other hand, had recently become *too much* of a morning person—she had taken to jogging every morning before heading off to her job as an advice columnist at the *Bay Mirror* newspaper. As a result Phoebe was up and out of the house by six thirty. Piper kind of missed having breakfast together as a family. Lately she and her sisters seemed to be living very separate lives.

By the time she got downstairs, the ringing had stopped. She pulled open the heavy wooden door and peered into the morning sunshine. Two people were heading down the walkway from the house—a dark-haired woman and a strawberry-blonde girl.

"Hello?" Piper called. "Can I help you?"

The woman turned back, her pretty face collapsing into an expression of relief. She grabbed the girl next to her—Piper figured she was about twelve or thirteen—and ran back up to the door.

"Are you one of the Charmed Ones?" the woman cried. "Please say you are."

Piper froze. That was a pretty abrupt question,

especially coming from a complete stranger. "Who's asking?" she replied suspiciously, taking a step back toward the relative safety of the Manor.

"I need your help," the woman said. "There's something terribly wrong with my daughter!"

Now that they were closer, Piper could see that the girl had been crying. Her face was blotchy and her eyes were swollen and red. But that didn't mean she and her mother weren't demons. Since there were always evil forces after Piper and her sisters, she had to be very careful, no matter how harmless these two looked.

"Why do you think I can help you?" she asked.

"You're one of the Charmed Ones," the woman said. "The most powerful witches there are."

Piper tried to keep a poker face. "Witches?" she repeated. "Who said we were witches?"

"I did a spell," the woman told her. "To ask for help. And it sent me straight to you."

Piper raised her eyebrows, surprised. "Are you a witch?" she asked.

The woman nodded. "I'm Juliana O'Farrell, and this is my daughter, Lily," she said. "We're *both* witches."

Piper narrowed her eyes. "Prove it."

Juliana's eyebrows shot up, and she looked at Piper suspiciously. "You want me to do magic right out here in the open?" she asked doubtfully.

"You want me to let you into my house when I

don't know anything about you?" Piper coun-
tered. She was acting tough, but in reality she was
beginning to feel that this woman was telling the
truth. Sometimes demons could pass as humans,
but there was usually something about them that
made Piper's skin prick a little. She got nothing
but good feelings from these two.

Juliana bit her lip, still regarding Piper with
suspicion. But then her daughter gave a little
sniffle. She looked ready to cry again, and
Juliana sighed. She glanced around, then pulled
a twig off one of the big bushes near the door.
Hiding the twig from the street with her body,
she focused on it and it burst into flames in her
hand. Quickly she blew it out. Then she glanced
up at Piper. "I'm a firestarter," she explained.
"It's my main power."

"Works for me," Piper said, holding the door
open wider. "Come on in."

She led Juliana and Lily into the living room.
So far Lily hadn't said a word. She just stared at
her feet. Piper felt sorry for the poor kid.

"So tell me about your problem," she said to
Juliana as they all sat down.

"It's not me, it's Lily." Juliana shot a worried
look at her daughter. "Her powers are missing."

"What do you mean, missing?" Piper asked.
She was already running through scenarios in
her mind—had a demon stolen Lily's powers?
Did she have some kind of power-sucking
parasite?

"In our family every girl receives her powers on her thirteenth birthday," Juliana explained. "It's been that way for generations. Lily turned thirteen yesterday."

"And no powers," Piper said.

Lily began to cry. Juliana fished a tissue from her bag and handed it to her. "Nothing. I can't understand it."

"I've been preparing my whole life for this," Lily sobbed. "What's wrong with me?"

"Don't worry, honey, we'll figure it out," Juliana promised. But Piper could tell this poor mom was just as worried as her daughter.

"Hey! What's going on?" Paige asked, coming into the living room. She looked only slightly more awake than before.

Piper introduced her half sister to the O'Farrells. "Juliana and Lily here have a problem," she explained to Paige. "Lily's powers were supposed to manifest yesterday. And it didn't happen."

"Bummer," Paige said sympathetically, plopping onto the couch next to the teenager.

"Do you think maybe they're just late?" Lily asked hopefully.

"Could be," Piper replied. "But the question is *why* they would be late."

"Do you have any enemies?" Paige asked Juliana.

The woman nodded. "One. A demon named Gortag."

"He's our family enemy," Lily put in. "For six generations he's been after us." Piper smiled. Lily sounded proud to be the one giving them information. She really *had* been preparing for witch-hood!

"Why is he after you?" Paige asked. "I mean, other than just being evil."

"Because our ancestor imprisoned him in a cave for fifty years," Lily said. "Then when he escaped, he got a warlock to put an enchantment on our family."

Piper and Paige exchanged a worried look. "What kind of enchantment?" Piper asked.

"There was an ancient prophecy that said the only way to vanquish Gortag is for a mother and daughter of the O'Farrell blood to combine their powers against him," Juliana explained. "So Gortag got the warlock to put a spell on our family . . . a spell to prevent women of the family from giving birth to girls."

Paige yawned. "Sorry, I think I'm still waking up," she said. "But I don't get it—if you can't have girls, how can the family continue?"

"Through the male line," Juliana explained. "Witches give birth to sons, the sons' wives give birth to daughters."

"As long as the daughter isn't born to an O'Farrell witch, it's okay," Lily put in. "The mother and daughter can't combine their powers if only one of them has inherited the family powers."

"But couldn't the sons just marry witches?" Paige asked. "Then they could have daughters and be mother-daughter witches."

Juliana shook her head. "One of my ancestors did marry a witch, and she had a daughter, but they were both killed in a fight with Gortag."

"So a witch who's not of your bloodline can't fulfill the prophecy, even if she has a daughter," Paige said. "That's a powerful enchantment."

Piper studied this mother and daughter, baffled. "Um . . . forgive me for stating the obvious, but you two don't seem to be following these rules."

Lily smiled for the first time, her whole face lighting up with pride. "Mom found a way around it."

"I thought I did," Juliana said. "I did a counterspell before I even got pregnant, and I chanted it every night until Lily was born. It took me two years to come up with the spell. I thought it had worked."

"And now?" Paige asked.

Juliana shrugged helplessly. "I wonder if something went wrong. Maybe my counterspell was strong enough to let me have a daughter, but not strong enough to let me have a witch for a daughter."

Lily began to cry again. This time Piper leaned over to the end table and retrieved a whole box of tissues. She handed it to the sniffling girl. "Has that ever happened before?" she asked. "A girl born in your family who wasn't a witch?"

"No." Juliana shook her head. "Every girl has had power, and some of the boys. Some people have had strong powers like mine, others just had minor abilities. But none of the girls were ever . . . powerless."

"And what about Gortag?" Paige asked. "He's been free for a long time now—does he ever come after your family?"

"All the time," Juliana said sadly. "We used to be a big clan. I had seven brothers and sisters. Now it's only me and Lily. Gortag destroyed the rest of them. When Lily was born, my last brother shielded us from him so that Gortag wouldn't find out that there was finally a daughter. He died fighting Gortag."

Piper stared at her, horrified. Juliana and Lily were the absolute last of their clan? "That's awful," she said. "I'm so sorry."

For one brief moment Juliana's face softened, but then she pulled herself back together. "Yes, it's awful. We tried to get help many times over the years, but no one came to our aid, and it was finally our undoing. Lily and I have been in hiding ever since my brother died. There was a great fire, and I let it be thought that I'd died in the fire. I couldn't risk Gortag finding out about me—or Lily." She gave a cold smile. "It took an emergency to make me reveal myself to you. And after we solve this, Lily and I will disappear again until she's old enough for us to face Gortag together."

Piper didn't know what to make of it. This poor woman had suffered an enormous loss, and she was here asking for their help, but Piper got the distinct impression that Juliana didn't trust them. Her last comment had made it sound as if Juliana considered their hiding place compromised by the Charmed Ones.

She decided to focus on the problem at hand. "But you think Gortag is unaware of you," she said. "So it's unlikely he's involved in Lily's missing powers."

"I don't know," Juliana admitted. "I haven't had even a hint of his presence since I left my old life. But he's a strong demon; maybe he's working some kind of magic on Lily. I just don't know."

"Well, that sounds like one nasty demon you've got," Paige said. "But we can take him."

Piper raised her eyebrows. "Oh, yeah?"

"Sure," Paige said confidently. "He's vulnerable to a mother and daughter team, right? Why wouldn't a three sisters team do the trick just as well, especially when those sisters have the Power of Three?"

"It may have to," Piper agreed. "But first I think we have to find out what's happened to Lily's powers."

Paige flipped through the Book of Shadows, humming to herself. It always felt good to help out an innocent, but helping an innocent who was also a witch was even better. She glanced over at Lily, who was sitting sadly on the old couch in the corner of the attic. Her mother was downstairs with Piper, scrying for Gortag.

"Hey, squirt, you wanna help?" she asked.

Lily shook her head.

"Come on, it'll be fun," Paige pressed. "We don't let just anyone look at our Book of Shadows, you know."

Lily shrugged. She didn't even bother to make eye contact.

Paige knew what that meant—her job in the Social Services department had put her in a position to see a lot of unhappy teens. And having been a teenage girl herself, Paige understood that no one could sulk quite as well as a thirteen-year-old who hadn't gotten her way.

"What did you do for your birthday?" Paige asked, trying to draw her out. "Have a party?"

"No, I just stayed home," Lily muttered. "We were supposed to stay inside until I could figure out how to control my new powers."

"Oh. Good idea," Paige said. *Duh.* How could she have asked such a thoughtless question? She tried to cover. "Well, I'm sure you'll have a huge party once we sort out this mess."

Lily looked unconvinced.

"So," Paige continued, "it was just you and your mom?"

"And my best friend. Drew."

"Really?" Paige was surprised. Why would Juliana let someone else be around when Lily was supposed to be receiving magical powers?

Lily shrugged again. "Drew's always there. She practically lives at our house."

Paige felt the hair on the back of her neck rise. Could this Drew person have something to do with Lily's missing powers? "Don't you spend time at Drew's house too?" she asked.

"Sometimes." Lily wrinkled her nose. "But her parents are really weird."

"Weird how?"

"They act like Drew shouldn't have any friends at all. Like she's just supposed to sit at home with them all day."

Paige nodded. "I had some friends like that when I was your age. Their parents don't realize they're growing up, that the most important thing to them is their friends."

"Maybe." Lily didn't seem to think that was the problem. "Anyway, my mom lets Drew stay as long as she wants after school."

Paige had a feeling Lily wasn't telling her the whole story about this girl Drew. She got the impression that Lily didn't tell her mother everything about Drew either. "She likes Drew?"

"She says the three of us are like peas in a pod," Lily replied. "She calls Drew her extra daughter. We all have the same eyes." She exaggeratedly batted her green eyes.

This information didn't sit right with Paige. It seemed odd that a woman with so much to hide—not only her own witchiness, but her daughter's, too—would let an outsider hang around so much. Juliana really hadn't seemed to trust people all that much. *Maybe she misses her big family*, Paige thought. Juliana had grown up with a lot of siblings. Maybe she wanted her only daughter to have something similar.

Still, it wasn't unusual for demons to take on human forms. Maybe this one had taken on the form of a teenager and stolen Lily's powers!

"Does . . . does Drew know about you and your mom?" she asked casually. "About you being witches?"

"No!" Instantly Lily shot up off the couch. Her cheeks turned red. "Do you mind if I look at your book now?" She hurried over and began studying the Book of Shadows.

That was a strange reaction, Paige thought. Was Lily lying, or was she just embarrassed? She'd have to mention it to Piper later. In the meantime she had a spell to find.

"What we need is a locator spell," she explained to Lily. "But not a physical locator spell. A . . . metaphysical locator spell."

"What does that mean?"

"Well, some locator spells find people or objects," Paige explained. "But we want a spell that will find your powers."

Lily nodded, still staring at the book. "This is

cool," she whispered. "We don't have anything like this in my family."

"But you seem to know a lot about your family history," Paige said.

"Mom has been telling me stories ever since I can remember," Lily told her. "She wanted me to realize how important it was—the craft. You know, so I'd be ready when I got my powers."

Paige felt sorry for the poor girl. When she'd received her own powers not all that long ago, she hadn't been ready for them at all—she hadn't even known that her birth parents had been a witch and a Whitelighter. So suddenly having magical powers had been sort of difficult to adjust to. But Lily was still just a kid, and she'd spent her whole life looking forward to the day when she would become a witch. Paige could only imagine how horribly disappointed she must be.

"Tell you what," she said to Lily. "Once we figure this out and get you your powers, you can come over and practice spells with me."

Lily's face lit up. "Really?"

"Sure. I could use the practice," Paige said. "I'm still pretty new at this myself." She turned her attention back to the Book of Shadows and found the spell she wanted. She quickly memorized the spell and glanced up at Lily. "Why don't you go call your mom and Piper?" she suggested. "We're ready to find your magic!"

• • •

"Lily, you stand in the middle," Piper said. She tried to smile reassuringly, but she was worried. She and Juliana hadn't found Gortag by scrying, but Piper couldn't shake the feeling that he was involved with Lily's missing powers. And he sounded like one seriously nasty demon. Anyone who could take out an entire clan of witches had to be pretty formidable.

Lily took her place in the center of the attic. Piper joined hands with Paige and Juliana, forming a circle around Lily. "Ready, everyone?" she asked. They began to recite the incantation:

> *Goddess, your daughter stands before you,*
> *But her magic has fled.*
> *Help her find what she has lost,*
> *That she with her magic may be wed.*

A white light appeared on the ground at Piper's feet. As they repeated the spell, the light began to move around the circle, going faster and faster until soon it was just a blur. The light spread into the center of the circle and climbed up Lily's body, surrounding her in light.

It was working! Piper watched closely, waiting to see where the light went next. It was supposed to lead them to Lily's magic, wherever it was. Piper half-expected the light to lead them to a demon's trap, so she wanted to be on guard.

The white light rose to the level of Lily's head. And then it faded.

"What's happening?" Paige whispered.

The white light slowly sank back down to the ground and went out, disappearing into the floorboards. Piper stared at it as it vanished. What was going on? Were they supposed to follow the light downstairs? She looked up at Paige. "Was that supposed to happen?" she asked.

Paige frowned. "I don't think so."

Piper let go of Paige and Juliana's hands. "It felt as if the spell just died halfway through," she said. Paige nodded in agreement.

"Why would that happen?" Juliana asked. "Is it because your sister's not here?"

Piper thought about that—maybe they did need the Power of Three. "We can try it again when Phoebe gets home," she said. "But I don't think that's the problem."

"Then what is the problem?" Paige asked. "Because this fizzling-spell thing is kinda freaking me out."

Piper looked at Lily, who was still standing in the center of the room, hugging herself as if she was scared. The poor girl seemed on the verge of tears again. Piper didn't want to upset her any more, but she had to say what she thought.

"I think the spell didn't work because we asked it to look for Lily's powers. And she doesn't have any. That's why it just died away."

"But we knew my powers were missing," Lily said nervously.

"We assumed they were missing—that maybe

someone had taken them, or hijacked them or something," Piper said. "In that case your powers would still be out there somewhere. But it seems like . . . it seems like your powers are just gone."

Chapter 2

Phoebe ran up the last few steps to the front door of Halliwell Manor and stopped, trying to catch her breath. This jogging every day thing wasn't nearly as much fun as training to kick butt, Charmed-style, was. But running was a good way to clear her mind—not to mention make sure her toned figure *stayed* that way. And it did sort of invigorate her. As she pushed the door open she felt ready to take on anything that came her way.

"Phoebe! You're back!" Paige said as soon as Phoebe walked inside. "We need you to do a spell with us." She thrust a piece of paper into Phoebe's hand, then yanked her into the living room.

"Whoa!" Phoebe cried. "No 'Good morning, how are you, I made coffee'? Just 'Say this spell'?"

"Good morning, how are you, I—uh—didn't make coffee," Piper said, dragging Phoebe to the circle they were forming with some strange woman around a kid. "Just say the spell now, please? I'll explain later. We think it might need the Power of Three."

"Okay," Phoebe said. She took her sisters' hands and tried to read off the slip of paper at the same time.

> Goddess, your daughter stands before you,
> But her magic has fled.
> Help her find what she has lost,
> That she with her magic may be wed.

A white light began glowing around their feet, then died out. They stopped chanting.

Phoebe glanced around at the glum faces. Paige and Piper looked confused, the woman was clearly worried, and the teen girl seemed ready to have a tantrum. "Well, that wasn't your usual Power of Three," Phoebe said. "Maybe because we had a fourth."

"Maybe your magic isn't as strong as you thought," the strange woman said, frowning at her.

Phoebe frowned right back. How dare this woman question the Power of Three! "Who are these people and what are they doing here at this hour of the morning?" Phoebe glared, her demon radar at work.

"This is Juliana O'Farrell and her daughter, Lily," Piper said. "They're witches."

"Out for an early morning stroll? Just thought you'd stop by because . . . ?" Phoebe didn't want to be so suspicious, but it wasn't often the Power of Three fizzled without the interference of a very powerful demon.

"I'm not," Lily muttered, "just stopping by. Or a witch."

"Oh, honey, of course you are," Juliana told her. Phoebe noticed that when she spoke to her daughter, Juliana seemed much less suspicious and much more normal. "You're just having a bumpy start."

Paige nodded. "Don't worry, Lily, we'll have you witching it up in no time. We just need to figure out the problem first."

"So I'm guessing from the spell we just did that Lily's powers are MIA?" Phoebe said. "Did we check the usual suspects?"

"There's a family enemy by the name of Gortag," Paige told her. "A demon. But he hasn't shown his face yet."

"And he's never stolen anyone's powers before," Juliana put in.

"Maybe he learned a new trick," Phoebe suggested.

"We did some scrying, but no major evil is showing up this morning," Piper said. "And the locator spell isn't finding a trace of Lily's powers anywhere. If Gortag stole her powers yesterd chances are he would've stuck around to attack."

Phoebe decided it was time for a Charmed Ones–only discussion. "Um, will you guys excuse us?" she said to Juliana and Lily. "We just need to talk for a minute."

"Is there a bathroom for Lily to wash her face?" Juliana asked.

"Sure." Piper pointed the way to the powder room.

As Phoebe followed Piper toward the kitchen, she heard Juliana talking to Lily. "It's time to stop crying now," she was saying sternly. "We don't even know these people—they could be dangerous. You're showing a weakness by crying. Go wash up."

Wow, thought Phoebe. *Kind of harsh for a mom. And how dare she think we're dangerous!* She glanced over her shoulder to see Juliana settle herself on the living room couch. She didn't look happy.

In the kitchen Phoebe opened the refrigerator and pulled out a bottle of water. "So what's really going on?" she asked quietly. "Because when we did that spell, I couldn't feel a trace of power coming from Lily. And Juliana's acting really distrustful."

Piper chewed her lip thoughtfully. "I agree."

"I mean, are we sure this girl is supposed to have powers?" Phoebe pressed. "Her mom's not trying to scam us or anything?"

"They come from a long line of witches,"

Paige said. "Why would the line suddenly break with Lily?"

"What does Leo think?" Phoebe asked.

"I haven't called him yet," Piper said. "It seemed like a fairly simple case of misplaced powers. But now I'm worried that this is something bigger."

"Well, I'm not convinced that this Juliana person is telling us everything," Phoebe said. "Leo!"

Her brother-in-law orbed in immediately. He looked around at the three of them with a smile on his face. "Morning, everyone," he said. "What's the problem?"

Phoebe pointed to their guest in the living room. Juliana stared back at them with a look of disgust on her face, taking Phoebe by surprise.

"Uh, hi," Leo called. "I'm Leo. I'm Piper's husband."

"You're a Whitelighter," Juliana spat.

They all stared at her in surprise. "Yes, I am," Leo said. "Is that a problem?"

Juliana hesitated, then shook her head. "I need to check on Lily," she said shortly, heading toward the powder room.

Phoebe raised her eyebrows. "Okay," she said. "That was weird."

"So I'm guessing you want me to find out about her, huh?" Leo said. "And what her problem is with Whitelighters."

Piper was frowning. "She doesn't trust us, and she obviously doesn't trust you." She gave her husband a pat on the arm. "But I believe that she really needs help. Why else would she risk coming to us when she clearly isn't happy about it?"

"I agree," said Paige. "And Lily's really bummed about not getting her powers."

Phoebe hadn't thought of it that way. It was true that Juliana didn't seem to want to be there. She must have a good reason.

Piper quickly filled Leo in on the O'Farrells' situation. "Right. I'll see what the Elders have to say," he told them, preparing to orb.

"And find out what they know about this Gortag guy too," Phoebe put in.

"Got it." Leo orbed out in a stream of white light. Phoebe sighed. "I'll call the office and tell them I'm working from home this morning."

"And I think I feel a bad cold coming on," Paige said with a grin. "Wouldn't want to spread the germs."

"So do we have a plan?" Phoebe asked.

"I think we need to find Gortag," Piper said. "He didn't show up through scrying, but I bet if you did a spell to call him, he'd come. Especially if he can tell that Juliana is here."

"So let's call him and vanquish him," Paige stated matter-of-factly.

"We can't vanquish him right away," Piper said. "First we have to find out if he took Lily's powers."

Phoebe frowned. She wasn't sure she loved the idea of setting a trap for a demon. "But Lily is vulnerable without her powers," she pointed out. "You guys can defend yourselves, and hopefully Juliana can too. But Lily's just a kid."

"That's why we have to keep Gortag away from her," Piper said. "She's safer here, so you should cast the summoning spell at Juliana's."

"Okay. Why'd you say 'you' not 'we'?" Phoebe asked her.

"I'm going to keep an eye on Lily," Piper announced. "Here, where it's safe."

"This is boring," Lily complained. "Why can't we go to my house?"

"Because if someone managed to steal your powers yesterday, that means they knew where to find you," Piper explained.

"So?"

"So your home isn't safe for you until we figure out what happened."

Lily rolled her eyes. "My mother is there."

Piper took a deep breath, reminding herself that Lily was probably frightened. "Your mom may not be powerful enough to protect you," Piper said. "That's why we're not going to leave you—or her—alone until we catch our bad guy."

"Oh, please." Lily rolled her eyes again. She turned her back on Piper and stared sullenly out the kitchen door to the backyard.

I guess the conversation is over, Piper thought.

She'd figured it might be fun to keep an eye on Lily for a while. She hadn't spent much time around kids lately, and since she and Leo were talking about starting a family soon, she'd hoped it would give her some practice. But she'd forgotten that thirteen-year-olds weren't exactly kids anymore. Lily had an opinion on everything, most of them unfavorable. She didn't want to watch TV because daytime shows were lame, she didn't want to learn about making vanquishing potions because the herbs were smelly, and she didn't want to do her homework because school was for losers. Piper suspected that Lily didn't really feel this way, and she knew Lily wouldn't say these things in front of her mother. She was just acting out. But that didn't make it any easier to deal with.

Piper turned back to her vanquishing potion. "Are you sure you don't want to help?" she asked without much hope. "I know you're upset that you didn't get your powers. But you can make potions even if you don't have any powers!"

Lily shrugged without turning around.

"Have you learned about magical herbs from your mom?" Piper pressed, determined to engage the girl.

"Yeah," was all Lily said.

"It sounds like she's done a good job getting you ready to be a witch," Piper said. "I'm a little jealous. Our mom didn't even tell us we were witches."

That caught Lily's attention. She turned ever
so slightly toward Piper. "Why not?"

"I think she was worried that we'd feel as if
we didn't have a choice," Piper tried to explain.
"She wanted us to be whatever we dreamed of
being. And if we knew we were witches, we
might feel as if we couldn't follow our other
dreams. But mostly I think she didn't want to
put us in danger."

Lily scuffed her shoe along the floor. "My
mother doesn't care about putting me in danger," she said. "All she cares about is having a
witch daughter to help her get rid of Gortag."

Piper caught her breath. Was that true?
Juliana had seemed to distrust the Charmed
Ones, but Piper hadn't thought the woman was
that awful. "Don't you think that maybe the reason your mom trained you so well was to make
sure you could defend yourself?" she asked.
"Not just against Gortag, but against anything
that could come your way?"

Lily snorted. "No. Why do you think she
dragged me here to you guys? She's been waiting her whole life for me to get my powers so
that we could go back and avenge her brother's
death. She thinks she has to make up for all the
other people in our family who Gortag killed."

Piper tried to imagine being the last member
of her family alive. It was too horrible to con-
template. It was almost too overwhelming
when she lost one sister to evil. She simply

wouldn't entertain the thought that anyone else in her life would meet the same fate. Especially not her sisters, or Leo.

She suddenly realized that Juliana had never even mentioned a husband or a boyfriend. "Where's your father?" she asked Lily softly.

"Who knows?" Lily said. "He left when I was a baby. Mom says it's because he was too young to handle the responsibility. But I think he probably resented me. Like, once I was born, Mom and I were the strong ones. She didn't need anyone else."

"Wow," Piper said. "That's a pretty harsh thing to say." She knew adolescent girls usually had rough patches in their relationship with their parents. But this seemed extreme.

Lily looked a little ashamed of herself. "I guess," she muttered. "It's just . . . I feel like my mom has been expecting so much from me. I've been learning about the craft ever since I can remember."

Finally she was opening up! Piper tried to play it cool, knowing that Lily would clam up again if she made a big deal of this. "And?" she asked casually.

"And I don't get it," Lily admitted in a whisper.

Piper was surprised. "What do you mean?"

"I'm supposed to be a witch, right?" Lily said in a rush. "And I'm supposed to inherit some kind of magical power. But I don't feel like a witch. I don't think I *am* a witch!"

Piper smiled. "What do you think a witch

feels like?" she asked. "Because I think we feel just the same as everybody else."

"But you have all this power," Lily argued. "I mean, my mom can start fires with her mind, and I thought that was a lot of power. But you and your sisters are so much stronger than that. You've probably saved the world, like, a hundred times."

"I think it's still in the double digits," Piper replied. "But you're right, my sisters and I are powerful when we're together. Just like you and your mother will be."

"But what if we're not?" Lily asked. "What if I never get my powers? Or if I get them and my power is something lame, like . . . well, like . . ."

Piper laughed. "See? You can't even think of an example. That's because *all* witchy powers are pretty cool."

"But if all I can do is create a bad smell or something, I'm not gonna be much help when Gortag shows up looking for a fight."

She had a point. It did seem like a lot of pressure on a girl so young. Piper tried to sound reassuring. "Well, the combination of powers is always stronger than just one witch, no matter what the individual powers are."

"But what if the legend isn't true?" Lily asked. "What if it's just a legend, and my stinky power—or whatever it is—turns out to be too lame to get rid of the demon?"

"That's why we're making a vanquishing

potion," Piper said. "Hopefully we'll take care of Gortag for you."

"Whatever." Lily stared out the back door again. Piper sighed. It was exhausting talking to a teenager! One minute she was right there with you and the next . . . who knew? She could only imagine how Juliana must feel. Trying to concentrate on the potion, she ran through possible ingredients in her mind. It was different every time—what killed one demon might make another demon stronger. And she didn't know much about Gortag—usually she found it easier to come up with a vanquishing potion after she'd actually seen and fought with the demon.

"Burdock root," she murmured, searching through the cabinet. She didn't see it. "Hey, Lily, can you do me a favor?" she asked, pushing aside a tin of dried bay leaves to check behind it. "I think I left the burdock root drying up in the attic. Would you go see?"

Lily didn't answer. Annoyed, Piper pulled her head out of the cabinet and turned toward the teenager.

Lily was gone.

Piper stared around the empty kitchen, shocked. She hadn't even heard the girl move! But the kitchen door was ajar and there was no sign of Lily anywhere. Piper ran over and yanked open the door. The backyard was the same as ever. Lily wasn't there. Piper took a deep breath. "Leo!" she called.

Her husband appeared almost immediately, orbing in amidst a swirl of white light. Piper couldn't help feeling a little tingle at the sight of him. She'd been in love with Leo since the very first day they met. Sometimes she still couldn't believe they'd overcome so many difficulties and actually gotten married. He caught her eye and grinned. "Miss me?" he asked.

"Yes," Piper said, giving him a quick kiss. "But I'm missing someone else, too."

"What do you mean?" Leo asked.

"Lily's gone," she said.

Leo frowned. "Do you think someone took her?"

"No." Piper hadn't sensed any other presence, evil or otherwise. "I think she ran away."

"What? Why would she do that?" Leo asked.

"She wasn't very happy," Piper said. "I thought it was just typical teenage behavior— you know how kids that age hate everything."

"But now?" Leo prompted.

"Now I think I probably should've paid more attention to her," Piper admitted. "She was complaining about how much pressure she was under. But I thought she understood the danger. It never occurred to me she'd take off."

"If she feels pressured, she might be trying to escape," Leo agreed. "Would she go home?"

"I doubt it. Her mom is the one putting all the pressure on her," Piper said. "Did you find out anything about them?"

"Nothing you're going to like," Leo said grimly.

"Why not?" Piper asked.

"The Elders won't help Juliana and Lily," Leo told her. "The O'Farrells turned their backs on the Elders. Juliana refused her Whitelighter's assistance."

"What?" Piper cried. "Why? When?"

"When her family was killed," Leo said. "Apparently there was a fire. Her Whitelighter came to orb her and her baby to safety and Juliana refused. She blamed the Elders for letting Gortag kill the rest of her clan."

Piper's mouth dropped open. "And so the Elders have just washed their hands of her?" she demanded. "She was alone and angry because her whole family had been murdered! She couldn't possibly have been thinking straight!"

"I agree," Leo said. "But Juliana renounced her connection to the Elders and to her Whitelighter. They had to respect her decision. All they can do is wait for her to return to them on her own."

"So they can't help us at all?" Piper said. "Can they tell us anything about Gortag?"

"Not much," Leo said. "They told me the same prophecy about him—that he'd be killed by the combined powers of a mother and daughter. The O'Farrell clan tried to get the Elders to help them with Gortag before, but the Elders couldn't reverse the enchantment the family was under. All they'll say about Gortag is that he's extremely strong and resilient."

"Resilient?" Piper repeated. "What's that supposed to mean?"

"That's just what Phoebe said when I orbed over to tell her about it," he said with a half-smile.

"Juliana did say her family had once asked for help and not gotten any," Piper said thoughtfully. "She probably hasn't forgiven the Elders for not being able to save any of them. I guess that's why she's so mistrustful. She truly feels that she and Lily are alone in the world." She glanced up at her husband. "I want to help them. Maybe we can convince them that they aren't friendless."

"So we'll help them," Leo said firmly. "I'm going to make Juliana like me no matter what!"

Piper smiled. It was hard to imagine anyone not liking Leo. "You'll help even though the Elders won't?" she asked.

"Yup," he said. "Maybe I can convince her to seek a reconciliation with them."

"Okay, so we're on our own," Piper said. "Can you sense Lily?"

"I'll try." Leo concentrated for a moment. He frowned. "I'm not getting anything. Are you sure she's our innocent?"

"Positive," Piper said. "It's either her or her mother." She gazed at Leo, concerned. Why couldn't he see where Lily was? Could it have something to do with her missing powers? Maybe a demon took her and put some sort of magic shield around her. . . .

"Wait! I've got her," Leo said suddenly. "She just got off a streetcar downtown."

"Is she all right?" Piper asked.

"Yeah. She seems fine," Leo said. "She just met another girl her age."

"Well, they're both in for a surprise," Piper said. "Let's go." She took Leo's hand and he orbed them downtown.

Lily spotted them right away—Piper saw her green eyes widen in surprise. She grabbed the dark-haired girl next to her and started to turn away. But Piper wasn't about to let her get away again. She jogged the ten feet between them and stepped in front of Lily. "Going somewhere?" she asked.

"It's none of your business," Lily muttered. "I was bored at your house." She was trying to act tough, but Piper could tell Lily was ashamed of running away. Her pale cheeks were flushed a bright red.

"Let's go," the other girl said urgently, pulling on Lily's arm. Piper glanced at the girl, startled to discover that up close her hair was a deep shade of blue. But her eyes were just as green as Lily's.

"I don't think so," Leo put in, stepping up behind the two girls. The teens looked at Leo in surprise.

"Who's that?" Lily asked.

"I'm Piper's husband, Leo," he said. "And you must be Lily." He held out his hand for her to shake. Lily's flushed cheeks turned almost purple as she took his hand. Piper couldn't help smiling—Leo was pretty cute, after all. Even a thirteen-year-old could see *that*. "And who's your friend?" Leo asked, turning to the blue-haired girl.

Piper watched as the two teens exchanged a worried look. "This is Drew," Lily murmured. "My best friend."

"Can we go now?" Drew asked anxiously.

"No, Lily can't go anywhere today," Piper said sternly. "I need her to stay where I can see her."

"It will just take a minute," Lily protested.

"*What* will just take a minute?" Piper asked.

"I have to go to the ATM," Lily said. "I owe Drew money."

"You came downtown to go to the bank?" Leo asked skeptically. "Why couldn't you just pay Drew back at school tomorrow or the next day?"

The two girls exchanged another worried look. There was more going on here than either of them was admitting. But what? Piper couldn't imagine what could be important enough to Lily to make her willing to leave the protection of a Charmed One. Didn't she understand that there could be demons—or worse—after her?

"I'm . . . um . . . I'm going away," Drew mumbled. "So I needed the money today."

Piper turned her attention to Drew, who immediately looked down at her sneakers. Her shoulder-length blue hair fell forward over her face, hiding her expression. "Why aren't you in school today, Drew?" Piper asked.

"Lily's not in school," Drew pointed out.

"Lily has a good reason for skipping today, and she has her mom's permission," Piper said. "And besides, I was asking about *you*, not Lily."

Drew didn't answer. Lily looked terrified. Piper sighed. "Are you cutting class, Drew?" Piper asked.

Drew nodded.

"Were you planning to run away?" Leo asked gently.

There was a long pause. Then Drew nodded again. Her big green eyes filled with tears. "Don't tell on her! Please don't tell her parents!" Lily cried, putting a protective arm around Drew's shoulders. "She'll get in so much trouble."

"I have to tell her parents," Piper said. "Running away is a big deal. Drew could've put herself in danger without even realizing it."

"No, we had it all planned," Lily said. "I was going to give her enough money to take a bus up to her grandma's house in Sacramento."

"Can't you just let me go?" Drew asked. "I'll be fine."

Piper glanced up at Leo. His forehead was

creased with worry. "No, you can't go all the way to Sacramento alone," he said. "We're going to take you home. We'll talk to your parents."

"They're gonna kill me," Drew wailed.

"Please don't tell them!" Lily begged again.

Both girls seemed on the verge of hysteria. Piper didn't know what to make of it. "Why are you so afraid of your parents?" she asked Drew.

"Because of my hair," Drew cried. "They're gonna kill me."

Piper couldn't believe it. All this because she dyed her hair blue? "Come on, Drew, it won't be that bad," she said reassuringly. "They might be mad that you colored your hair, but you can just dye it right back to its normal color. They'll get over it."

Drew and Lily both gave her an unmistakable "you-don't-get-it" look. And Piper thought they might be right—maybe she *didn't* get it. Both girls seemed way too worried about Drew's parents. Dyeing your hair seemed like a pretty minor offense. But maybe Drew's parents were very strict.

"Okay, I know your parents won't be happy," Piper said. "And you'll probably be in a lot of trouble—maybe you'll even be grounded. But it's better than running away."

"Yeah, right," Drew murmured. Piper looked to Leo. He shrugged helplessly. Piper wasn't sure what to do. But Lily was under her care, and she had to step up and be the adult in this situation.

"Well, let's get you home, and then Lily and I will head back to the Manor." Piper tried to sound upbeat, but really she had no idea what she was going to say to Drew's parents, or how she would even explain who she and Leo were. She'd just have to figure that out as she went.

Piper turned to lead the way, then stopped abruptly. She and Leo had orbed here. They had no car! It was fine for Lily to know about the orbing, but Drew had no idea there was a whole world of witches and Whitelighters. How were they going to get her home?

"Um, I'll call a cab," she said, turning back with a smile. She pulled out her cell phone.

"I live two blocks away," Drew said. "I'll just walk home."

"No, we'll go with you," Leo said. Drew opened her mouth to argue, but Leo's expression stopped her. Without a word, she led the way to her apartment building and up the stairs to the fourth floor. She unlocked the door to apartment number 7 and stepped inside. As Piper followed she took in her surroundings. The building was a nondescript townhouse with a few bushes planted out front. The hallways were clean and well lit, with cheap industrial carpeting. And the living room of Drew's apartment was small and spare but had sunlight streaming through the windows. It seemed like a perfectly nice place.

"Mom?" Drew sounded nervous. "You home?"

From the buildup the two girls had given of Drew's parents, Piper was expecting a scary taskmaster of a woman. But when Drew's mother appeared from the kitchen, Piper found herself looking at a pretty, middle-aged woman with a sweet smile. "Well, hi," she said, looking around at the group. "What's all this?"

Drew stared at the floor. So did Lily. *I guess it's up to me,* Piper thought. "Um, hello, Mrs. . . . ," she faltered, realizing she didn't know Drew's last name.

"Elson," the woman said. "Are you from the school?"

"No," Piper told her. "I'm Piper Halliwell. I'm a friend of Lily's."

"Oh." Mrs. Elson looked confused.

"Um, this is my husband, Leo," Piper went on in a rush. "We know Lily's mother."

"Okay." Mrs. Elson still seemed baffled. "Is there a problem?" She glanced at her daughter. Drew didn't meet her eye.

"Well, Lily was spending the day at my house, but she snuck out to meet your daughter," Piper started.

"Drew! You're a bad influence on Lily," Mrs. Elson cried, suddenly angry. "Go to your room!"

Drew shuffled off. Piper, surprised, watched her go. Where had that change in Drew's mother come from? "I didn't mean to imply that it was Drew's fault," she said quickly. "She was worried that you might be mad at her because of her hair, so she was thinking of running away—"

"Thank you for bringing her home," Mrs. Elson cut in, her smile back in place. She walked over to the door and opened it. "I'm sorry if she's interrupted your day."

Piper and Leo exchanged a confused look. They didn't seem to have much choice. "You're welcome," Piper said, leading the way out. In the hallway, she turned back to Mrs. Elson. "If you need any help—," she began.

But Mrs. Elson had closed the door in her face.

Piper stared at the gold number 7 two inches from her nose. "Well, that was rude," she said.

"I told you her mother sucks," Lily muttered.

"Yes. She does." Piper narrowed her eyes at the girl. "But she's not my problem. My problem is that Drew was planning to run away and *you* were planning to help her. Don't you see how dangerous that is?"

"She can take care of herself," Lily protested.

"Piper means it's dangerous for you," Leo put in. "You're unprotected without your powers. If someone took them from you, they did it in order to leave you vulnerable."

"It's nice that you want to help your friend, Lily," Piper said. "Even though you should never help someone run away. But you have to try and understand how serious your situation is. Promise me you're going to stay put from now on."

"Okay," Lily said.

"Good. Let's go home." Piper took Leo's hand. He grasped Lily's elbow and orbed them all out of the hallway.

Chapter

3

Paige followed Juliana and Phoebe into the
O'Farrells' cottage and locked the door behind
her. It never hurt to be careful when you were
planning to do magic. Juliana was already pushing aside the coffee table in the small living
room to make space for their spell. They were
going to summon a demon, and demons could
take up a lot of room.

"Hey, what kind of demon is Gortag, anyway?" she asked. Leo hadn't been able to tell
them much when he orbed into their car on the
way over. She could still remember how
annoyed Juliana had looked when he appeared.

Juliana shrugged. "Far as I know, nobody
ever lived long enough to document him. All
they ever passed down was the warning. When
he attacks, run or he'll kill you."

Phoebe was frowning. "He must be a fast demon.

I have to say, I don't understand it," she told Juliana. "You seem like a pretty powerful witch, and your whole family has always had magical ability. Why hasn't anyone managed to vanquish this guy?"

"I'm not sure," Juliana admitted. "It's as if he has some sort of power over witches when he gets near them. They just stop fighting."

Paige didn't like the sound of that. "You mean he hypnotizes them or something?"

"It's hard to say," Juliana replied. "The stories about Gortag came down to us from ancestors who had seen from a distance the destruction he caused. No one who got close to him lived to tell why they weren't fighting back."

Paige shot Phoebe a look. "I think we're going to need a cage," she said. "We're gonna want to contain as much of his power as we can."

"Gotcha," Phoebe replied. "Juliana, do you have any crystals?"

"Of course. They're in there." Juliana pointed to an elaborately carved wooden chest in a corner of the room. "We call that the magic box. It's been in my family for more than a hundred years."

Juliana was beginning to relax a little around them, Paige thought. She was trying to see Juliana's side of things. After hiding for so long, it must be hard to suddenly open up your life and your home to three strange witches.

Phoebe crossed the room to open the chest.

"Why don't you guys have a Book of Shadows?" Paige asked Juliana. "You seem to have so many family traditions and stories. Didn't anyone ever write them down?"

Juliana laughed. "One of our family traditions was that we could never write anything down," she said. "There was an old belief that if you put a spell on paper, it could be used against you. Plus, three of our ancestors were burned at the stake during a witch hunt in Ireland. After that, it was forbidden to have records of our craft."

"Yeah, our ancestors had some experience with that too," Paige said. "Isn't it strange? We both come from long lines of witches, we live in the same city . . . why haven't we ever heard about you guys before?"

"I told you, we were hiding," Juliana said, her defenses snapping back into place.

"Even from people who could help you?" Paige wasn't sure she understood that.

"Maybe once Lily is older, and she's able to defend herself from evil things, I'll stop hiding," Juliana said. "But ever since she was born, protecting her has been my first priority. And that meant keeping quiet about being a witch." A worried tone crept into her voice as she spoke.

"Are you sure that Lily hasn't told anyone about your heritage?" Paige asked. She couldn't help wondering about Drew, the friend Lily had told her about.

"Of course she hasn't!" Juliana sounded shocked at the idea. "I've taught Lily everything about being a witch—including the fact that most mortals are afraid of us and most demons want to kill us. There's danger everywhere."

"But you know how kids are," Paige pointed out. "They all think they're indestructible."

"Not Lily," Juliana said firmly.

Paige decided to drop it. She'd seen how differently Lily behaved when her mother wasn't around. But clearly Juliana thought of her daughter as a good little girl, not a complicated—and unhappy—teenager. And it wasn't Paige's place to correct her. Besides, they had more important things to worry about.

"How's the crystal cage coming?" she called to Phoebe.

"I think these will do." Phoebe had found four large white quartz crystals in the magic box. She arranged them on the floor in the center of the room, forming a square. "All we have to do is get Gortag to step into the square. Then we can activate a cage."

Paige sighed. It was the best they could do, but she still wasn't thrilled. Getting a violent and powerful demon to step into a cage wasn't going to be easy.

"Okay, let's call our demon," she said. "Did you bring the spell, Phoebes?"

Her sister nodded. "One Gortag-summoning spell coming up," she said, pulling a scrap of paper out of her jeans pocket.

"Are you sure this is the best idea?" Juliana asked nervously. Paige could imagine how she felt.

After hiding from a monster her whole life, they were expecting her to call him into her living room.

"It will be fine," Paige said reassuringly. "You've got us to protect you. We've vanquished more demons than I can count."

Juliana took a deep breath. "You guys are brave," she said. She gave them a hesitant smile. "I'm sorry I seem so prickly. I haven't been around other witches in a long time. I . . . my family didn't really trust anyone but O'Farrell witches. We were very tight-knit. We didn't like to let outsiders in."

"Well, we're here to help," Phoebe said simply. "And you're going to have to trust us."

Juliana nodded. "Okay, I'll try. And I'll try to be as brave as you too."

"I mostly just fake the brave part," Paige confided, sharing a smile with her sister.

"That's all bravery really is," Phoebe added. "You do what's needed, even if you're scared."

Juliana bit her lip. "Let's do it," she said.

Paige took her hand, then joined hands with Phoebe. Phoebe held the scrap of paper out in front of them, and they all read aloud together:

Fire and earth, hear our command!
We summon a demon from the dark lands.
Gortag, come!

The first thing Paige noticed was the stench— a smell like rotten eggs mixed with horse poop.

It filled the air as soon as they stopped speaking. Phoebe gagged. "What *is* that?" she cried.

"Gortag," Juliana said, her face white with fear.

"*Gross*-tag is more like it," Paige muttered. "I can smell him, but where is he?"

"I am here!" a voice boomed. The air in front of Paige blurred, as if someone had blown a giant soap bubble and she was looking through it. The bubble grew larger . . . then popped. In its place stood a skinny, five-foot-tall demon with red skin, a long pointy tail, and curved horns on his head. Paige's mouth dropped open.

"You must be kidding me," Phoebe said, echoing Paige's thoughts. "You look like a kid dressed as the devil for Halloween."

Gortag turned to face Phoebe, fixing his yellowish eyes on her. "You will not mock me," he said.

Phoebe nodded. "Right. Sorry. I will not mock you."

Paige snorted. "*I* will," she said. "You don't look very fearsome." She turned to Juliana. "Is this really Gortag?"

Juliana shrugged helplessly. "I've never seen him. I've only seen the destruction he leaves behind."

Paige didn't know what to think. This demon seemed like a joke. He was so small that she could take him on her own, and she didn't even have the martial arts training that Phoebe had.

How could he have terrorized an entire clan for generations? "Well, let's get him in the crystal cage, just in case," she said.

Gortag looked back at Phoebe. "Protect me," he commanded.

"I don't think so," Paige said, stepping toward him. Phoebe leaped forward and delivered a roundhouse kick, knocking Paige to the floor.

"Hey!" Paige yelled. "That hurt!"

Phoebe's eyes widened. "Paige, I'm so sorry," she gasped. But then she whirled around and shoved Juliana, who was rushing at Gortag. Juliana fell to her knees.

"Phoebe!" Paige cried. "What are you doing?"

"I don't know," Phoebe said, horrified. "I just have to protect him."

"*What?*" Paige said, shocked. Had her sister gone crazy?

Gortag studied Juliana as she climbed back to her feet. "This is an O'Farrell witch," he said conversationally. "I thought I felt the energy of your wretched family in the spell that called me."

Juliana narrowed her eyes, and Gortag's tail burst into flame. Phoebe dove on it, smothering the fire with her jacket. Gortag didn't even seem to notice. He took a step closer to Juliana. Paige watched him carefully—he was only a foot away from the square that marked where the crystal cage was. She inched forward, ready to push him into the middle of the crystals.

Phoebe stood up, blocking her way.

"Phoebe, move," Paige said.

"I can't. I have to protect Gortag," Phoebe replied. She looked as annoyed as Paige felt.

"Why?" Paige demanded.

"Because he told me to," Phoebe said. "I can't help it. I have to listen."

Gortag ignored the sisters, keeping his eyes on Juliana. "I thought I had killed the last of your clan," Gortag said. "This is an unexpected pleasure."

"Stay away from me, you jerk," Juliana muttered. She set his hand on fire. Gortag chuckled. He raised his flaming hand and formed a fist. The tongues of flame curled around his clenched hand, forming itself into a ball of fire. He threw the fire back at Juliana. She screamed and ducked.

"Fireball!" Paige cried, orbing the ball of flame into the fireplace. Phoebe turned to watch it. *Now's my chance*, Paige thought. With all her strength, she hurled herself at her sister, knocking her onto the couch. Paige fell on top of Phoebe and tried to hold her down.

"Juliana!" she yelled. "Get him!"

While Phoebe was distracted, Juliana grabbed a fireplace tool and swung it at Gortag. Startled, he stepped back—into the square of crystals.

White light shot simultaneously from all four crystals, forming a magical cage around Gortag. He bellowed in anger, but now that he was safely contained, he didn't seem so imposing anymore. Paige glanced down at Phoebe, who was still fighting to get up.

"What is with you?" Paige demanded.

"I think he put a spell on her," Juliana said breathlessly, running over to help hold Phoebe down.

Paige studied her sister's face. She hadn't heard Gortag say a spell, but Phoebe certainly wasn't acting like herself. "Goddess, hear my call. Release!" she said.

Immediately Phoebe stopped struggling. "Finally," she said. "What a relief!"

"What happened?" Paige asked. "How did he manage to put a spell on you without us hearing it?"

"He just looked into my eyes," Phoebe said, making sure to avert her gaze from where Gortag paced about the tiny crystal cage. "And I had to do whatever he said. It felt as if he spoke right into my mind."

"That must be how he did it," Juliana said. "How he made my ancestors stop fighting him."

"You mean he's just psychic?" Paige asked skeptically. "That's his big power?"

"I've never felt anything like it before," Phoebe said. "He's not just run-of-the-mill psychic—it's as if he put a piece of himself in my head. I knew I didn't want to be fighting you, but somehow I just had to. He was making me."

Paige glanced over at the scrawny red demon,

careful not to meet his eye. "It's hard to believe he's so strong," she commented. "I guess you can't judge a demon by its appearance."

"So what are we going to do with him?" Juliana asked.

Paige still held on to Phoebe's arm. "Are you sure you're done being Gortag's protector?" she asked.

Phoebe nodded. "I promise."

"Okay." Paige released her sister. "Don't look at him again."

"Don't worry," Phoebe murmured. "I'm not looking for any more sisterly smackdowns." She sat up and rubbed her arms where Paige and Juliana had been holding her.

"Well, I guess we should question him," Paige said. "That's the whole reason for not vanquishing his butt, isn't it?"

"Remember, don't meet his eye," Phoebe warned as they all turned toward the crystal cage—and the angry demon inside.

"Release me!" he commanded.

"Sorry, shortie," Phoebe replied. "I'm not under your control anymore."

Gortag stood very still. Paige could tell he was staring at them, willing them to meet his eye. Just knowing that someone was looking at her made her want to look back. To keep from accidentally glancing up at his face, she concentrated on his kneecaps. They were knobby and red, just like the rest of him. She still couldn't get her mind around the fact that this scrawny little devil was a dangerous and deadly foe.

"Look at me!" he bellowed, his frustration erupting in a burst of violence. When none of them complied, he hurled himself against the walls of the crystal cage. The crystals had created a sort of force field, so Gortag seemed to be bouncing off of empty air. After a few tries, he dropped to the floor. He did it so quickly that Paige found herself looking down into his face before she realized what had happened.

"Aah!" she cried, shutting her eyes. She turned to the side before opening them again, just in case Gortag was still staring right at her.

"This is harder than I thought it would be," Juliana said from beside her.

"I know," Paige agreed. "Let's just ask him about Lily's powers, fast."

"Tell us what you did to Lily," Phoebe demanded.

"Why should I?" Gortag replied.

"Because we'll vanquish you if you don't," Paige told him.

"You'll vanquish me anyway," Gortag said.

Paige glanced at her sister. "He has a point," she said.

"But I'm willing to make a deal," Gortag added. "I'll tell you what you want to know if you set me free."

"Well, I suppose I could orb him someplace far away from us," Paige said with a wink at

Phoebe. Maybe if they played along, they could convince Gortag that they'd deal with him. She had no intention of really letting him go.

"I'm sick of this," Juliana said suddenly. She ran to her family magic box and pulled out a jeweled knife. "Do you recognize this?" she demanded, storming right up to the crystal cage. She didn't look Gortag in the eye, but she pointed the knife at his chest. "My ancestor used this knife to draw her own blood for the spell needed to imprison you in that cave for half a century. I'll do the same spell and send you right back there."

Her voice was strong and her words threatening, but Gortag just laughed. "You stupid witch," he said. "Your family hasn't been keeping very good track of me, have they? I destroyed that cave the minute I got free. I doubt you even know the spell she used to trap me there."

Paige shot Juliana a questioning look. Juliana shook her head. Gortag was right—Juliana didn't know how to trap him again. Paige couldn't blame her for trying to bluff him, though. And it gave her an idea. Juliana was already playing "bad cop." Paige might as well try playing "good cop."

"Look, Gortag," she said. "Let's be reasonable. You've been after the O'Farrells for years. That means we'll have to vanquish you . . . unless you tell us what we want to know. Now, what did you do to Lily?"

"What makes you think I did anything to Lily?" Gortag asked.

"Her powers didn't manifest," Phoebe said. "The only one who would benefit from that is you."

"I don't know what you're talking about," Gortag insisted.

"Just tell me what you did to my daughter," Juliana growled.

"*Daughter?*" Gortag cried. "You have a *daughter*?"

Paige had to admit, Gortag sounded shocked to hear that Lily was Juliana's daughter. And if he hadn't even known she existed, he couldn't have been the one to steal her powers.

Juliana looked horrified. She'd spent her whole life trying to hide Lily from this guy, and now she was the one who'd alerted him to Lily's existence. "Don't worry," Paige told her. "You have nothing to fear from Gortag—we'll keep him in the cage until we figure this out. Then we'll vanquish him."

"So after all these years, there's an O'Farrell mother and daughter," Gortag said. "I knew that warlock's magic wasn't strong enough to last."

"It lasted for six generations," Phoebe told him. "That's longer than *you* should've lasted."

"And your little girl is missing her powers?" Gortag asked. "Maybe she doesn't have any to begin with."

"She does," Juliana snapped. "We all do. And

as soon as we find hers, she and I are going to destroy you just the way you deserve."

Paige was looking at Gortag's tail. The very end flicked back and forth the way a cat's did when it was hunting. *That's not good*, she thought. What was he up to?

"I think we should just vanquish him now," she said aloud. "We know he's not the one who took Lily's powers. There's no reason to keep him around."

"I agree," Phoebe said. "We can use Juliana's kitchen to make a potion."

But Gortag had begun to laugh. It was a deep sound, almost a growl, that filled the entire room. "You can't vanquish me!" he cackled. "You don't even know where I am!"

"We're looking right at you," Juliana pointed out.

"Gortag has many bodies!" Gortag trumpeted. "Destroy this one. It will not hinder me at all!"

"What's he talking about?" Phoebe cried, turning to Juliana.

"I have no idea," Juliana admitted.

"What do you mean, you have many bodies?" Paige demanded. "Where are all the others?"

"They are out there," Gortag said, his voice sinking to an evil whisper. "Linked together by my mind. They all know what I know now . . . that the O'Farrell witches have a daughter."

"His mind!" Phoebe said, dismayed. "He's

telepathic. I felt how powerful his mind is."

"You felt only a tiny piece of my mind," Gortag spat. "My bodies are out there now, all guided by one powerful will. And all are focused on one purpose." He smiled at Juliana. "To find your daughter while she is powerless. And to kill her."

Chapter
4

"Did we look in the Book of Shadows for him?" Phoebe demanded, driving as fast as she could toward Halliwell Manor.

"Yeah," Paige told her. "I didn't find anything. Since he has so many bodies, maybe he also has a bunch of different names."

"What does that mean, anyway?" Juliana asked from the backseat. "How can he have many different bodies?"

"Maybe he's bluffing," Paige said hopefully. "He wanted us to think that vanquishing him wouldn't work."

"I don't think so," Phoebe replied. "I felt how powerful his mind is. He wasn't bluffing about that." She shuddered as she remembered the sensation. It hadn't been as simple as hearing his voice in her head. It was more like he had taken over her body and made it do things she didn't want to do. "Maybe he takes over the bodies of other demons—or mortals—and uses them however he wants," she said. "That could be what he means."

"I can't believe Leo couldn't find out more about him from the Elders," Phoebe complained.

"Well, they were right about one thing," Paige replied. "He's resilient—because he has more than one body."

"Your Whitelighter won't help," Juliana said with a sneer. "The Elders and their Whitelighters never helped us."

Phoebe glanced in the rearview mirror and met Juliana's eye. "Look, lady, I don't know what happened between you and your Whitelighter," she said. "But Leo's our family. If you've decided to let us help you, that means you have to let him help you too."

Juliana squirmed uncomfortably. "My Whitelighter didn't try to save my brother from Gortag," she said. "He would only help me, because I was his charge and my brother wasn't."

Ouch, thought Phoebe. "I'm sorry," she said aloud. "But Leo isn't like that. In fact, most Whitelighters aren't like that at all. It sounds like your experience was terrible. But we're gong to show you that most good magic can be trusted."

Juliana nodded stiffly. "I understand that you're close to Leo. But I don't think he can help us. You've heard for yourself what little information he got about Gortag."

"Research takes time," Paige said. "The Elders haven't let us down yet. We'll get to the bottom of this together."

"I don't even want to think about what would've happened if Lily had been there," Juliana said. "I'm glad she's safe with your sister."

Piper glimpsed the living room through the white light as Leo orbed her and Lily back to the Manor. As soon as the light faded, she spotted the demon—a small red guy with horns and a tail.

He rushed straight at Lily.

Leo grabbed her hand and orbed her away as she started to scream.

Left alone, Piper turned to the demon and raised her hand to explode him. She looked into his yellow eyes as she threw her power at him. Before the power hit him, Piper had the strangest feeling that he was talking to her— some kind of mind-to-mind communication. Then he exploded.

Leo orbed back in with Lily, who was still screaming.

"It's okay! It's okay!" Piper cried, rushing to comfort Lily. She'd been behaving like such a brat since her mother left that Piper had almost forgotten Lily was still just a kid. Just because she'd learned about demons all her life didn't mean she was prepared to see one running right at her. "I got him," she assured Lily.

The girl looked up at her, wild-eyed. "Where is he?"

"I exploded him," Piper explained. "It's one of my powers."

Now Lily looked at *her* fearfully. "You can blow people up?" she asked.

Piper nodded. "At first all I could do was freeze them—you know, sort of stop them in their tracks. But over time I developed the ability to explode them too." Lily still looked frightened.

"She only does it to bad guys," Leo added.

Lily glanced around the room as if she expected the demon to jump out from behind the couch and attack her again. "Was that a demon?" she asked.

"Yup," Piper said.

"What demon? Who was he?"

"I don't know," Piper said. "I didn't stop to chat before I got rid of him."

"He looked like . . . the devil," Lily whispered.

"Yeah, I guess he did," Piper replied. "You'll get used to it. Demons come in all shapes and sizes."

"Phoebe was married to one," Leo said.

"Leo!" Piper couldn't believe he wanted to gossip about her sister's love life. But when she caught sight of Lily's face, she realized that Leo was on to something. Lily was incredulous, her fear forgotten.

"No way!" she cried. "Your sister married a demon? Did he look like that guy?"

"No," Piper said, smiling. "He was only a half-demon, and he was actually pretty cute. I mean, in his demon form he was scary looking, but usually he just looked like a regular guy."

"That's why you can never tell who's a demon and who's not," Leo told Lily. "You have to be on your toes."

Lily nodded. "That's what my mom is always telling me," she said. "But I never really knew what she meant before."

"Once you're a full-fledged witch, you'll start to develop instincts about people," Piper said. "You'll be able to figure out who's on your side and who's not. At least most of the time." She led the way into the kitchen. "Anyone hungry?"

"Actually I have to go," Leo told her. "One of my charges has been calling me for the past few minutes."

"Okay. Thanks." Piper gave her husband a kiss and smiled as he orbed out of the kitchen.

"How come my mom and I don't have a Whitelighter?" Lily asked.

"I dunno." Piper tried to keep her voice light. Obviously Juliana had never told Lily about her decision to renounce her Whitelighter. Piper didn't even want to try to explain a decision like that. She began getting veggies out of the fridge to make a salad. "Maybe because your mother was trying to hide you, she dropped any contact with her Whitelighter." There. That was close enough to the truth.

Lily sighed. "I wish I had known about you guys sooner," she said. "You're so brave about being witches. Mom always makes it sound like some big shameful secret."

"I'm sure she was just trying to protect you," Piper said. She felt sorry for Juliana, who had had to hide her real nature for so long. But she could also sympathize with Lily, who had never had an example of a strong, fearless witch on whom to model herself.

"So why was that demon here, anyway?" Lily asked. "What did he want?"

Piper hesitated. "I'm not sure," she admitted. She'd been so busy trying to calm Lily that she'd pushed the strange demon right out of her mind. "I've never seen him before. Lots of demons come after us—they want to test their power against the Charmed Ones."

"Maybe we should look him up in your Book of Shadows," Lily said.

"Good idea," Piper told her.

"Can I go look in the book right now?" Lily asked excitedly.

"Knock yourself out," Piper said with a smile. "I'll come join you when the salad's done."

"Okay." Lily ran off upstairs, and Piper began chopping carrots and snow peas to make a salad. She'd barely started when the phone rang. She grabbed it off the counter and stuck it between her ear and her shoulder so both hands would be free to keep chopping.

"Hello?"

"Piper, it's me!" Phoebe said. "Is Lily okay?"

"Yeah. Why?" Piper asked. But her sister's answer was lost in static. Phoebe's cell phone must have cut out. Piper looked at the half-finished salad and sighed. She'd better go up and check on Lily. She wiped her hands and headed up the wide staircase. As she reached the landing, she heard a strange thumping noise from upstairs. Alarmed, she jogged up the stairs to the attic.

"Lily?" she called, pushing open the door. But Lily was nowhere to be found. "Lily!" she yelled, frantically looking around the messy attic. How could she have been so stupid? A demon had just attacked them in her own living room—why did she ever let Lily out of her sight?

Then Piper noticed the open window. She ran over and peered outside. Lily was climbing down the latticework at the bottom of the porch. She must have climbed all the way down from the attic. Piper couldn't believe it. Lily was running away *again*.

"Lily! Stop right there!" she yelled.

Startled, Lily did stop. She was on the ground now, under the big maple tree on the front lawn. She turned back toward Piper, and for the first time Piper could see that she held the Book of

Shadows in her arms. Piper gasped, horrified. Lily tried to run, but the Book of Shadows pulled her back. Piper could see the girl having a little tug-of-war with it. She wasn't worried about the book—it couldn't leave the Manor. The magic on it was strong; it knew how to protect itself. But just the fact that Lily would try to steal it was unacceptable.

"That's it," Piper muttered. She raised her hand to freeze Lily. But Lily was too fast. When she saw Piper preparing to use her powers, she let go of the Book of Shadows and ran. Piper froze the maple tree mid-sway in the wind.

Piper let out a grunt of frustration. She was the worst baby-sitter in history! Lily had given her the slip two times in one day. Piper waited only long enough to see the Book of Shadows float easily back up into the attic and settle itself on its podium. Then she went after Lily.

As Piper ran back down the two flights of stairs, she debated whether or not to call for help. Lily's trying to take off with the Book of Shadows was a bad thing. But calling Leo or her sisters would mean admitting that a thirteen-year-old had outsmarted her . . . again. And she had a pretty good idea where Lily was heading.

Piper snatched her car keys from the table in the foyer and ran out the front door. With any luck she'd make it to Drew's apartment before Lily did.

• • •

"I can't get any service," Phoebe complained. She was so busy staring at her cell phone that Paige was afraid she'd drive off the road.

"Don't worry," Paige said, taking note of a yellow light up ahead. "We're almost home." She pointed at the traffic light and Phoebe hit the brake.

"Sorry," Phoebe murmured.

Paige glanced at Juliana in the backseat. She didn't want to alarm their innocent, and Phoebe's crazy driving just might do exactly that. "Phoebes, you okay?" she asked. "Do you want me to drive?"

Phoebe shook her head. "I'm feeling a little strange, that's all. I think I have a magic hangover from Gortag messing with my mind."

"That really got to you, huh?" Paige was surprised. Phoebe had been through so much in the short time Paige had known her—an ex-demon husband, an evil pregnancy, being the Queen of the Underworld. One little psychic demon shouldn't be enough to rattle her.

"It was just such a weird sensation," Phoebe admitted. "I know I'm overreacting. It feels as if he zapped my brain with electricity, and now I'm still having little aftershocks."

Paige was looking at Phoebe, but she caught a glimpse of something red from the corner of her eye. Someone had just run out in front of the car!

"Look out!" Paige yelled. Phoebe slammed on the brakes and swerved to the side of the road—just as a small red demon leaped up onto the hood of the car.

"It's Gortag!" Juliana cried.

Phoebe put the car in park and began unbuckling her seat belt. "Set him on fire!" she ordered Juliana. Juliana narrowed her eyes, and Gortag's horns began to spark. He shook his head, and the flames flew off him like droplets of water.

"Keep trying," Paige told her. Phoebe was climbing out of the car, and Paige figured she'd better follow. She had a feeling that Phoebe was going to try to fight him hand-to-hand, and she had to watch her sister's back. But it would be easier to take on a demon who was distracted by being on fire.

Juliana's eyes were filled with tears. "He's too strong," she said, panicked.

Paige had no time to be sympathetic. "No, he's not," she said bluntly. "There are three of us, Juliana. You just have to be brave."

The poor woman looked terrified. But Phoebe was outside now, and Gortag got the first blow. Paige winced as her sister fell against the front of the car with a loud thud. It couldn't be easy trying to fight a demon without looking at his face, but Paige knew they couldn't risk making eye contact with Gortag or he might use his psychic powers on them.

"Juliana, fire!" Paige yelled as Phoebe ducked under another blow.

Juliana concentrated, and Gortag's entire tail burst into flames. He turned, startled, and Phoebe delivered a powerful roundhouse kick to his chest. He tumbled backward, landing on his tail. Immediately the fire spread, shooting up his spine until his entire body was on fire.

Paige scrunched up her face as she watched. She hated demons, but all of the violence was still upsetting to watch. But Gortag suddenly began to laugh. He looked straight at Paige, and before she could tear her eyes away, the demon changed. His yellow eyes lost their life. The red body went limp and collapsed like a rag doll. But Gortag's laughter went on.

The flames continued to burn the red body, but there was no demon in it anymore.

Paige shot Phoebe a worried look. "I guess he doesn't take over other people's bodies after all."

Phoebe was still breathing hard from the fight. "No. He really seems to have a bunch of different bodies that he can use and discard."

Juliana climbed from the car. "What happened?" she asked. "I heard him laughing even after he died."

"He didn't die," Phoebe said. "He just left that body."

"You mean he's a spirit, not flesh and blood?" Paige asked.

Phoebe shrugged. "We need to do more research."

The three women silently got back into the

car. Paige was worried. An in-the-flesh demon she could fight. But one who could jump from body to body, one who existed mainly in spirit form? That was a different story. She was beginning to understand why Juliana's family was so frightened of Gortag.

Piper stormed down the hallway to Drew's apartment and pounded on the door. As soon as she found Lily she was going to give her a no-holds-barred lecture. How could the girl not realize how much danger she might be in?

Drew's mother opened the door, a sour expression on her face.

"Mrs. Elson, I'm looking for Lily," Piper said.

"She's not here," the woman replied, beginning to close the door.

"I think she is, whether you know it or not," Piper said. She pushed the door back open and stepped inside. Piper hated to be so rude, but she couldn't take the chance that anything might happen to Lily. "Lily ran away again, and the last time she did that she went to meet Drew."

"Drew's not here either," Mrs. Elson said coldly.

Piper gaped at her. "But I just dropped her off here an hour ago," she said.

The woman shrugged.

"I told you Drew was trying to run away this morning," Piper said. "And you just let her leave?"

"She's a bad seed, that one," Mrs. Elson said. "She does whatever she wants." Piper thought she detected a hint of pride in the strange woman's voice.

"Are you telling me you let her run away?" Piper demanded. "Was Lily with her?"

"I haven't seen Drew since you brought her here," Mrs. Elson said. "When I went to check on her in her room, she was already gone."

"Where's her room?" Piper asked.

"Just who are you, anyway?" Mrs. Elson looked Piper up and down, a suspicious gleam in her eye.

Piper didn't know how to answer that one. "I have to check Drew's room," she insisted. She crossed the living room and headed down the hallway where she'd last seen Drew.

"I'm calling my husband," Mrs. Elson announced.

Guess I'd better hurry, Piper thought. She did feel bad about barging into the Elsons' apartment. But she couldn't help thinking they weren't the best parents to Drew. She was more worried about Lily, whom she'd only known for a few hours, than they were about their own daughter!

Piper opened the first door she came to. It was a bathroom, and it was empty. Closing that door, she went on to the next one. She twisted the doorknob, but it was locked.

"Lily?" she called. "Drew?"

There was no answer. The hallway only held one more door, so she tried that one. Bingo! This was clearly Drew's room—it had a twin bed, a small pink dresser, and photos of boy bands stuck all over the walls.

Piper stepped inside and quickly scanned the room. There was no sign of Drew—or Lily. The closet door stood open, revealing a few T-shirts and some jeans hung haphazardly on hangers. Not much of a wardrobe for a young girl.

A cool breeze hit Piper's cheek and she turned to the window. It was open wide enough for a person to climb through. Piper hurried over and looked outside. To her surprise, there was no fire escape. They were four stories above the sidewalk. It was impossible that Drew had gotten out that way. So where was she? And more importantly, where was Lily?

"You looking for my daughter?" A gruff voice interrupted her thoughts. A tall, heavyset man was standing in the doorway. He didn't seem happy to see her.

"You must be Mr. Elson," Piper said. When he didn't answer, she rushed on. "Actually I'm looking for your daughter's friend. Lily."

"Drew doesn't have any friends," he told her.

Piper had no idea what to say to that. This big man and his strange wife were making her uncomfortable, and she knew she had no business being in their apartment. Still, she was going to tell Paige to arrange a Social Services visit to this place, pronto.

"Lily was with Drew earlier today," she explained, edging around him toward the bedroom door. "I thought she might have come to see her again."

"Drew is a juvenile delinquent," he said bluntly. "She's been in trouble since the day she was born. If this Lily girl is hanging around her, it's bad news. I wouldn't be surprised if they both ran away."

Piper made it to the bedroom door and escaped into the hallway. She rushed back into the living room with the Elsons at her heels. "Well, I'm sorry to bother you twice in one day," she said. She yanked open the front door and stepped outside.

"If I find Drew, I'll call you," she said. But Mr. Elson just smirked at her as he closed the door.

Piper turned away, shaking her head. How could the Elsons be so casual about their own daughter's welfare? She pulled out her cell and dialed Phoebe's number. Her sister answered on the first ring.

"Where are you?" Phoebe demanded.

"I'm looking for Lily," Piper admitted. "She keeps running away. I thought I could handle it on my own this time, but she wasn't where I thought she'd be. We'd better call Leo."

"Piper!" Phoebe sounded horrified. "How

could you let her out of your sight? Gortag is after her!"

"What?" Piper was shocked at the level of fear in Phoebe's voice. "I thought you were going to set a trap for Gortag and keep him contained."

"We did," Phoebe replied. "But he has lots of different bodies, and he controls them all with some kind of psychic power."

"What are you saying?" Piper said, beginning to jog as she reached the stairs.

"I'm saying that there could be hundreds of Gortags out there right now," Phoebe told her. "And they're all looking for Lily."

Chapter
5

"Well, did it say anything about blue hair?" Drew whispered. She didn't want to draw any attention to her and Lily. The librarian had already given them a strange look when they walked into the public library in the middle of the afternoon on a school day.

Lily frowned. "I didn't see anything about blue hair," she admitted. "It's hard to remember. It was a big book."

Drew gave a growl of frustration. She'd been looking in witchcraft books for almost an hour, but she hadn't found anything to help her. She'd been counting on Lily to bring her the Halliwells' Book of Shadows. "I can't believe you just left it there," she complained.

"It wouldn't move," Lily insisted. "It was enchanted or something."

Drew pushed the witchcraft book away in

disgust. "This is totally useless," she complained. "What am I supposed to do now?" She pulled a strand of her deep blue hair in front of her eyes and twisted it around her finger. The color was actually pretty cool. But her mom had freaked out when she saw it. Drew had come out of her room where she was hanging with Lily, and her mom took one look at the hair and started screaming. She acted as if Drew had turned herself into someone else instead of just changing her hair. She'd thrown Lily out and locked Drew in her room.

Lily started flipping through the book Drew had discarded. "We could ask Piper and her sisters," she said casually. "They're the most powerful witches in the world. They must know how to dye your hair back."

Drew's mouth dropped open. Why hadn't she thought of that? "Let's go buy some brown dye at the drugstore," she said. "Do you have any money?"

"A little." Lily frowned. "But we can't go to my house or to your apartment or we'll get caught."

"We can dye my hair in a bathroom at the mall," Drew replied.

"Maybe . . . maybe we should go to the Halliwells' place," Lily suggested.

Drew immediately moved her chair away from Lily's. "No way," she said. "You saw how Piper treated me—like I was some kind of freak."

"But their whole job is to help people," Lily argued.

"Their job is to help *you*," Drew said. "Not me." She pushed back her chair and stood up. "I'm going to the drugstore," she announced.

"What are you gonna do, *steal* hair dye?" Lily asked.

"If I have to," Drew told her. "Are you coming or not?"

Lily stared at her, her green eyes worried. "I'm not even supposed to be *here*," she said. "They told me not to leave Halliwell Manor."

"Fine. Go back and hide," Drew said huffily. "I don't need you anyway." She turned and stormed off, trying to hide her fear. She always tried to act tough, like a loner. But without Lily's help she didn't know what she would do.

Paige chewed on her fingernail as she watched Juliana pacing. At the moment Juliana was one very pissed-off witch, and Paige couldn't blame her. She'd come to them for help, and instead they'd summoned a powerful demon who wanted to kill her and her daughter. Then they'd announced to the demon that her daughter was powerless. And then they'd lost her daughter.

"We'll find her. I promise," Phoebe said lamely from her perch on the arm of the couch.

Juliana shook her head. "I should never have left her alone," she muttered.

White light filled the living room as Leo orbed in. He took in the unhappy faces and grimaced. "Where's Piper?" he asked.

Paige shot him a "be quiet" look, but it was too late. The mention of Piper's name sent Juliana into a fury.

"Piper is out somewhere *not* finding my daughter," she snapped. "She let Lily run away, and now she can't find her."

"Wait a minute," Leo said. "Lily ran away *again*?"

Juliana stopped in her tracks. "What do you mean, again?"

"She ran away this morning," Leo said. "She just took off and went to meet her friend. Drew."

Juliana's cheeks flushed bright red. "Lily has never run away before," she said, defending her daughter. "Maybe she just didn't understand that you wanted her to stay here."

Paige couldn't help thinking about her conversation with Lily in the attic. She'd gotten the impression that Lily was a lot wilder than her mother knew.

"No, she definitely knew she was misbehaving," Leo told Juliana. "Her friend was trying to run away for real—up north somewhere. And Lily met her to give her money for the bus."

"I find this all very hard to believe," Juliana said stubbornly. "Lily is a good little girl."

"That might be the problem," Paige put in, trying to keep her voice neutral. "Lily isn't a little girl anymore. She might be dealing with things you don't know about."

Juliana sank down on one of the overstuffed chairs. "I *do* know that Drew is a troubled girl," she said. "Her parents don't seem to control her. But Lily has never followed her example before."

"I think she's started to today," Leo said. "Especially if she took off again after we brought her back here."

"Piper said something about wanting to handle it on her own," Phoebe put in. "I guess she thought she'd find Lily with this Drew girl. But she didn't."

"Can you sense her, Leo?" Paige asked.

Leo concentrated for a moment. "No," he said, a worried tone creeping into his voice. "That's weird. I could sense her this morning— that's how Piper and I got her back."

"Why would it change?" Paige asked. "If she's our innocent, you should be able to see her no matter what."

Leo shrugged helplessly.

Just then the front door banged open. Piper came rushing into the living room, her eyes searching for Lily.

"She's not here," Juliana said shortly.

Piper's face fell. "Oh, Juliana, I'm so sorry," she said. "If I'd had any idea that Lily would sneak out again, I never would have let her go up to the attic alone. I didn't even know anyone

could climb down those rickety old drainpipes."

"Well, Lily's still small," Phoebe said.

"She climbed down the drainpipes?" Juliana
repeated, surprised.

Paige felt for her—Juliana was learning a lot
about her daughter today that she hadn't known
before. She'd seen this type of thing before while
doing family counseling at work. Sometimes
even the most well-meaning parents didn't pay
attention to who their kids were becoming as
they grew up.

"Not only did she climb all the way down
from the attic," Piper said, "but she tried to take
the Book of Shadows with her."

"What?" Leo and Phoebe cried together.

Juliana turned white. "She tried to steal something from you?"

Piper nodded. "But it can't leave the Manor,
so it's okay."

Paige caught her breath. "Lily was really
interested in the Book of Shadows this morning," she said. "Do you think maybe she's trying
to do a spell herself?"

"To get her powers, you mean?" Juliana
asked.

Paige nodded.

"Wait, I got her!" Leo said suddenly. "She's at
the public library . . . with Drew. Should I orb in
and get her?"

"Not without me," Juliana said firmly. "I

want my daughter back where I can see her as soon as possible."

"Let's go, then," Leo said. He held out his hand to Juliana. She stared at it, still not trusting Leo. "It's the fastest way to get to Lily," he said softly. "Juliana, I'm trying to help."

Juliana seemed to come to a decision. She put her hand in his and they vanished into a cloud of white light.

Paige turned to her sisters. "Should we go too?"

"First tell me what's going on," Piper said. "I thought we were just dealing with a witch who'd lost her powers. But what's this about a bunch of different demons?"

"That's what I tried to call you about," Phoebe said. "But my stupid cell phone cut out."

"Technology just hasn't kept up with the demands of magic," Piper joked. "So tell me now. I don't know what we're fighting."

"Gortag is one demon," Paige explained. "But he has lots of bodies. He seems to control them with one mind."

"He's psychic," Phoebe added quietly. "His brain is seriously powerful. He made me fight Paige and Juliana to protect him."

"Did you vanquish him?" Piper asked.

Paige shook her head. "We left him in a crystal cage at Juliana's house. We figured the best way to make sure he's vanquished is to get Lily's powers back and combine them with Juliana's."

"I don't think he's vanquishable by normal methods," Phoebe said. "He attacked us later, in the car. And when we killed him, his spirit seemed to just drop his body. Like it was an out-of-fashion suit or something."

"Wait a minute," Piper said. "He doesn't look like a little mini-devil, does he?"

"Yeah, as a matter of fact he does," Paige replied. "How do you know?"

"He attacked us here, too," Piper answered grimly. "I exploded him right away. He didn't seem all that strong to me."

"Did you look in his eyes?" Phoebe asked.

"Just for a second while he was exploding," Piper said. "I did feel something a little weird, now that you mention it. Like a tingling."

"That's his psychic power," Phoebe said. "You're lucky he didn't manage to force his way into your mind—you would've turned around and attacked Lily yourself."

"How did he even know Lily would be here?" Piper asked. "I just assumed he was after *me*. Or us, for the Power of Three."

Phoebe's brow furrowed in concentration. "He put himself in my mind," she said slowly. "I bet he could see where I lived. He knew we were protecting Lily; he may have figured she'd be at our home."

"Makes sense." Piper glanced into the kitchen, where all the ingredients for her half-finished vanquishing potion were laid out next to those for her half-finished chopped salad. "I didn't complete a potion," she told her sisters. "But now I'm nervous about Juliana and Leo out there by themselves. I think we should go back them up in case Gortag shows his ugly red face again."

"Well, I'm taking myself out of this equation," Phoebe said. "Gortag has already been inside my mind. I'm afraid if I see him again he might be able to access my memories or something and find out how to hurt us or the O'Farrells. I could be a liability."

"Okay then, how about you stay here and write a vanquishing spell?" Piper suggested. "I'm thinking one verse to vanquish his bodies, another verse to vanquish his mind."

"Good idea," Paige said. "We'll be right back." Taking Piper's hand, she pictured the public library. Almost immediately she felt her molecules dissolve into a stream of light, carrying her and her sister instantly to the library.

Lily waited on the library steps, closely watching the crowds of people walking by on the sidewalk. One of these times, the person coming along would have to be Drew. Lily would run over to meet her, and Drew would pretend it was an accidental meeting, as if she were just walking back from the drugstore. But Lily knew Drew hadn't really gone to the store. For one thing, she didn't have any money. Drew did shoplift things sometimes, but usually only little stuff like gum or lip gloss. And besides, she wouldn't really leave Lily behind. They were best friends.

She hugged her knees to her chest. She felt bad about trying to take the Book of Shadows—she could still see Piper's furious expression in her mind. But Drew had told her to get a spell from the Charmed Ones, so she had done her best. Too bad the stupid book wouldn't leave home. She had to admit, though, the book was cool. When she'd glanced through it in the attic this morning, she had glimpsed spells to make two people fall in love, spells to call for ancestors and other witches, and lots of stuff about demons.

Lily shuddered, remembering the demon who had come running at her this morning. Had Piper really blown him up? Maybe she should get back to the Halliwells before Piper exploded *her*.

Lily glanced up at a squirrel in the trees on the library's front lawn. She narrowed her eyes, trying to make the squirrel levitate. Nothing happened. Lily sighed. Her grandfather had been able to levitate objects—that was his power, or so her mother said. Lily had spent all her life trying to imagine what power *she* would get when she turned thirteen. But she hadn't really known how many powers there were. She'd thought you could start fires like her mom, or you could levitate things, or you could maybe read minds a little like her old Aunt Romie. But since meeting the Charmed Ones, she had a

whole new opinion of witchy powers. They
were scary. The way Leo could orb through
space—and Piper had said Paige had that power
too. Or Piper, being able to freeze things. That
was serious stuff. And Phoebe could see the
future. Lily wasn't sure she wanted big, important powers like those. She didn't think she
could handle them.

She glanced back up at the tree. The squirrel
was gone.

"Hey," said a voice from behind her. Lily
turned to see Drew sitting two steps up.

"Where did you come from?" Lily asked, surprised. "I didn't see you walk up."

Drew just shrugged. But her face was pale,
and she didn't have her usual smirk. Lily could
tell there was something wrong. "Drew?" she
pressed. "How did you get here without me seeing you?"

Suddenly a white light flashed from behind
the tree. Lily jumped to her feet. That had looked
like the light from Leo orbing. Sure enough, Leo
stepped around the tree a moment later, followed by Lily's mother.

"Uh-oh," Drew murmured.

"I know," Lily replied. Her mom was going to
be really mad at both of them. But it was too late
to get away now. Leo was already on his way
over.

"Did he just do that orbing thing you told me
about?" Drew asked.

"Ssh!" Lily hissed. "You're not supposed to know about that!"

"Oh, right," Drew said. "And you and your mom aren't witches."

"Drew!" Lily cried. "You promised not to tell." Her mother was only ten feet away now, and if she knew Lily had spilled their family secret, Lily would be grounded forever.

"Whatever," Drew said. She stood up to leave.

"Hold it right there," Leo told her, jogging the last few steps over to them. "I want to talk to you both."

"Too bad," Drew said. "I don't want to talk to you." She began to walk away. But Lily's mother stepped up.

"Get back here, Drew," she commanded.

Drew turned and came back. Lily hid a smile—Drew acted so tough, but she always did everything Lily's mom told her to do. Lily thought Drew secretly wished Juliana were her mother instead of weird Mrs. Elson.

"I hear you tried to steal the Book of Shadows," Leo said. "I don't think you have any idea how important it is."

"Apologize to Leo, Lily," Juliana said sternly.

"Sorry," Lily mumbled. But she wasn't sure Leo even heard her, because a small red demon leaped in between them and attacked.

Piper looked around the nearly empty library reading room. She and Paige had orbed in between two bookshelves so that no one would notice them, but they shouldn't have bothered. It was a warm and sunny Wednesday afternoon, and no one was in the library.

"I don't see Lily," Paige said.

"Or Drew," Piper replied. "I was so sure that was why Lily ran away again."

"Don't be so hard on yourself," Paige told her. "You had no way of knowing Lily was a little con artist." She led the way through the reading room, looking under the big wooden tables to make sure their runaway wasn't hiding from them.

Piper followed with a sigh. It was true; Lily had completely fooled her twice today. She looked like such a sweet little girl, and she could act sweet too. But clearly the kid was used to charming her way into doing what she wanted.

"I don't understand why she'd want to steal the Book of Shadows," Piper said. "The first time she took off, she was obviously just trying to help Drew."

Paige stopped short. "Help Drew with what?" she asked.

"Her bizarro parents," Piper said, remembering the Elsons' odd behavior. "You seriously have to check out those people, Paige. Officially."

Her sister's eyebrows shot up. "Why? What's wrong with them?"

Piper thought about it. There hadn't been anything really *wrong* with Mr. and Mrs. Elson. But something about them had rubbed her the wrong way. "I'm not sure," she said. "They're strange. And they think their own daughter is a juvenile delinquent who has no friends."

Paige snorted. "I think they may be right about the delinquent part," she said. "And I'm afraid she's dragging Lily down with her."

"I think Lily just wants to help," Piper protested.

"I don't know," Paige said. "According to what Lily told me this morning, Drew was there yesterday when Lily was supposed to be getting her powers. And now Lily keeps running away, which Juliana says she's never done before. Plus, she tried to steal our book."

"So what are you saying?" Piper asked. "That Drew has something to do with Lily's missing powers?" She couldn't imagine someone so young having an evil agenda, but it was possible that Drew was some kind of demon in disguise.

"I don't know," Paige said. "All I know is, Lily's hiding something. And it's something about Drew."

Piper had looked under every table in the reading room. "They're not here," she said. "Let's go outside. Maybe Lily just left."

"Worth a try." Paige followed Piper to the revolving door at the front of the library. "It would be easier if Leo could still sense her."

"It would be easier if she'd stop running away," Piper replied. She pushed through the revolving door and stopped in surprise. Halfway down the front steps stood Leo and Juliana. And in front of them was Gortag!

Paige came through the door behind her. "Remember, don't look in his eyes," Paige said, starting to run. Piper charged after her down the steps toward the little group fighting the demon. Leo had shoved Lily and Drew behind him for protection, and Juliana was trying to set Gortag on fire. Piper raised her hand and exploded him from behind.

Before she had time to catch her breath, another Gortag appeared from behind a tall bush on the lawn. He rushed at them. Piper exploded him too.

"Get the kids out of here!" she called to Leo. Yet another Gortag was heading her way.

"I can't find Drew!" Leo yelled back.

"What?" Piper turned, confused. "She was standing right there a second ago."

"Well, she's gone now," Leo said. "Behind you!"

Piper ducked, and Gortag jumped over her. She set her hands in the center of his back and pushed as hard as she could. He toppled down a few steps, and Juliana set him on fire. But another Gortag was already on the way.

"He's after Juliana and Lily," Paige said breathlessly. "We have to get them to safety."

Gortag leaped at Juliana. Paige grabbed her and orbed them away.

"What about you?" Leo cried, worried.

"I'll be fine," Piper assured him. "Just come back for me soon."

Leo grabbed Lily and orbed away as the next Gortag attacked. Piper ducked under his blow. This was exhausting—and hard. She had to make sure her eyes never met Gortag's, but that meant her aim was a bit off. She accidentally exploded a backpack someone had left on the steps.

"You can't win, witch," the demon growled. "I have an endless supply of bodies at my disposal. I will wear you down."

"Not likely," Piper told him. "I think the cops will be here soon." She could see that a small crowd had gathered to watch the fight. Gortag looked so much like a guy in a devil suit that they probably thought this was some kind of performance art.

"I care nothing for such things!" Gortag crowed. "The petty mortals cannot kill Gortag! Let them come!"

Piper glanced at the shocked faces watching them. Gortag might not care if he was creating a scene, but she did. She didn't want to draw too much attention to herself. Exploding demons in a public place would be hard to cover up, even for the Halliwells' friend Darryl, a police detective. She made a break for the trees on the lawn.

As she ran she saw Paige and Phoebe orb in ahead of her. "It's about time," she said breathlessly. Gortag was right on her tail.

"Piper, duck!" Phoebe cried.

Piper dove to the grass, letting Phoebe execute a martial arts kick over her head. Gortag stumbled backward. Piper rolled over onto her back and exploded him. She braced herself for the next one. But nothing happened.

"Is it over?" Paige asked.

Piper climbed to her feet and scanned the lawn. "I don't see any more. Maybe he went after the O'Farrells."

"We'd better get back to the Manor," Phoebe said.

A few of the onlookers had followed them onto the lawn. "Yeah, and fast," Piper said. "I don't want any of these people to start asking questions."

They all ducked behind the tall hedge, and then Paige orbed them back home.

Chapter
6

Power of the witches, we call on you, come
Bring your power, protect our home.

Phoebe felt the familiar tingling feeling build as
she spoke the protection spell with Paige and
Piper. Magic coursed through them and radiated
out into Halliwell Manor itself. After the third
repetition, she knew the house was safe from
demon attacks, at least for a little while.
"Hopefully by the time Gortag figures out a way
around that spell, we'll know how to vanquish
him," she said breathlessly. They were all still
trying to catch their breath from the fight with
Gortag.

"We have to go back and get Drew!" Lily
cried, banging her small fist on the kitchen table.

Phoebe sighed. Lily must've said that ten

times already. The poor kid was hysterical. "Lily, we can't go get Drew when we don't know where she is," she tried to explain.

"You can find her!" Lily insisted. "You're witches, you can do a spell or something."

"Honey, Drew will be fine," Juliana said soothingly. "She's not in any danger. Gortag is after *you*, not Drew."

"She disappeared while you were fighting him," Lily pointed out, her panic rising. "Maybe one of his bodies grabbed her and no one noticed."

Phoebe chewed on her lip. Drew wasn't their innocent, but that didn't mean they could just let a demon grab her. "Is that possible?" she asked.

"I don't think so." Piper frowned. "It seemed as if every time I got rid of one Gortag, another one appeared. But I don't remember seeing two at once."

"That's true," Paige agreed. "I've only seen them one at a time too."

Phoebe felt a surge of hope. This could be the info she needed to help her write her Gortag-vanquishing spell. "So maybe he's not so all-powerful as he likes to say he is," she put in. "He might have an endless supply of bodies, but he can't use them all at once."

"If he could, he would've turned himself into an army by now and tried to take over the world," Leo said.

"So it's more like he just jumps from one

body to the next," Phoebe said thoughtfully. "I wonder where the new bodies come from."

"Maybe he's got a big closet full of devil suits somewhere," Paige quipped.

"You're probably closer to the truth than you think, Paige," Leo said. "I'd be willing to bet that when he leaves his current body, he's really transporting himself back into whatever dimension he came from."

"You mean a demon dimension?" Piper asked. "And that's where he keeps his extra bodies?"

"I don't think so," Phoebe replied. "If he just kept a bunch of bodies there, he could take as many as he wanted. He wouldn't need to use just one at a time."

"Well, maybe he can't control more than one body at any given time," Juliana suggested.

Phoebe thought about how Gortag had managed to invade her mind and force her body to fight Paige and Juliana. "I think he can control two bodies at once," Phoebe said. "He controlled *my* body and his own at the same time."

"Okay, so if he doesn't have a closet full of bodies in the demon dimension, what does he do?" Paige asked. "Just make a new one every time he needs to?"

"Maybe," Phoebe said. "Why not? If he's really going to another dimension, why couldn't he create a new body and then instantly pop back here? Time doesn't necessarily work the same way through dimensions."

"Who cares?" Lily yelled suddenly. She jumped up from the table. "I need to make sure Drew is okay!"

"Lily! Don't be so rude," Juliana reprimanded her. "The Halliwells are trying to help us. To help *you*."

How ironic, Phoebe thought. Juliana had sure taken her time deciding to trust the Charmed Ones, but she was certainly siding with them now!

"But I need to help Drew," Lily argued. "She's in trouble."

Phoebe saw Paige frown. "In trouble how?" Paige asked.

Lily looked down at her sneakers. She didn't answer. Paige sighed in frustration. Phoebe knew how her half sister felt. Lily was in a lot of danger, yet all day long she'd been worried about her friend instead of herself. Normally Phoebe would think that was noble. But under the current circumstances it was creating trouble. They couldn't seem to make Lily realize how vulnerable she was.

Phoebe pulled her chair closer to Lily's. The girl reluctantly sat back down. "Lily," Phoebe said sympathetically. "If Drew is really in trouble—if she's in *danger*—you have to tell us why. We can't help her otherwise."

Lily squirmed in her chair. "I don't know if it's *dangerous*," she said.

"If what's dangerous?" Phoebe pressed.

"I can't tell you," Lily said.

Phoebe rolled her eyes. "Fine. Then why don't you help us figure out how to vanquish Gortag," she suggested. "And then we'll get your powers back. And then we'll all go find Drew and help her however you want to."

"But what if she got hurt in the fight?" Lily asked. "You guys are supposed to help innocents, and Drew is just a kid and you're totally not helping her."

Phoebe bit back a sharp response. Lily was really starting to get on her nerves. She wouldn't let them protect *her*, but she was willing to play the guilt card to get them to protect Drew.

Unfortunately she had a point.

Piper stood up. "Tell you what," she said. "I'll go over to Drew's and make sure she's okay. If she's not there, I'll try to talk her parents into finding her. I'm old friends with them by now."

Lily's eyes lit up.

"There's one condition, though," Piper continued gravely, looking at Lily. "No more running away. You promise to stay here and let my sisters protect you."

"Okay," Lily said. "But you'll make sure Drew's all right?"

"Yup," Piper replied, heading for the door. "And by the time I get back, you guys will have figured out how to vanquish Gortag." She winked at Phoebe as she left.

Sure, no problem, Phoebe thought wryly. *One*

demon, an inexhaustible supply of bodies. Piece of cake!

"What about Lily's powers?" Juliana asked. "I know we need to get rid of Gortag, but he's not the one who stole her powers. We still need to figure out what happened to them."

"Just because Gortag says he didn't take her powers doesn't mean he's telling the truth," Paige said.

"He seemed pretty surprised to find out about Lily's existence," Phoebe said. "I hate to say a demon is telling the truth, but I kinda believed him."

"Me too," Juliana said. "And that means there's another explanation."

"I think Gortag is a more pressing priority," Phoebe argued.

"I'll work on finding out what happened to Lily's powers," Paige offered. "Phoebe, you and Leo and Juliana work on Gortag."

"Sounds like a plan," Phoebe agreed.

"Okay. We'll take the attic." Paige picked up the Book of Shadows, then headed up the stairs with Lily on her heels.

"So . . . Gortag," Phoebe said. "I've been trying to figure out whether to write a spell to vanquish his bodies or one to vanquish his mind."

"Maybe you can write a spell that will bind his mind to one body," Leo suggested. "That way if we destroy the body, we'll destroy Gortag himself."

"It's worth a try," Phoebe said. She grabbed her journal and a pen and got to work.

Piper knocked on the door of apartment number 7 and waited, bracing herself for the rude welcome she knew she would get. Drew's parents were not going to be happy to see her. She couldn't really blame them; all day long she had been bothering them. Whatever was going on with Drew, it certainly wasn't any of her business. But she'd promised Lily. And besides, Piper felt sorry for Drew.

The door opened, revealing Mr. and Mrs. Elson. They stared at her for a moment in silence.

"Hi," Piper said, trying to sound cheerful. "Me again."

"What do you want now?" Mr. Elson asked.

"I was wondering if Drew ever came home," Piper told them. "Because we found her with Lily, but then she . . . um, she must have run off again."

Drew's parents gazed back at her, unconcerned. Piper felt her cheeks flushing with anger. Didn't these people care about their daughter at all?

"I'm trying to make sure that Drew is okay," she said pointedly. "Is she here?"

The Elsons exchanged a look. Then Mrs. Elson held the door open wide, a smile crossing her face. "She's in her room," she said sweetly. "Would you like to check on her?"

Piper stepped inside, confused by the sudden change in the woman's tone. "I guess so," Piper said. "If it's not too much trouble. Lily will feel better if I tell her I saw Drew."

"Absolutely," Mrs. Elson said, leading the way to Drew's room. "Those two girls are so close—sometimes I tell them they should have been twins!"

Piper couldn't believe her ears. These were the same parents who had told her Drew didn't have any friends!

Mrs. Elson opened the bedroom door and gestured for Piper to enter. "You go on in," she said. Mr. Elson grinned at Piper from behind his wife.

Piper stepped inside. A quick glance showed her that Drew wasn't here. She whirled around to find that Mr. Elson was slamming the door in her face. Piper raised her hand to freeze him, but it was too late. The door was shut. She heard the lock turn. She was trapped!

Chapter
7

"Let's start at the beginning," Paige said as she led Lily into the attic. "Tell me all about what happened on your birthday." She set the Book of Shadows back on its podium and turned to Lily. She had no intention of letting the girl get away from her. Lily had already proven that she was slippery.

"I didn't go to school," Lily said. "Mom wanted me to stay home because she didn't know exactly when the powers would come."

"What time were you born?" Paige asked.

"Ten minutes before noon," Lily replied. "So Mom thought I might get my powers right then."

Paige nodded. That made sense. Her own experience had been pretty different—she hadn't received her powers until she entered Halliwell Manor after Prue died. One thing she did remember, though, was that there had been a forty-eight-hour window of time after becoming a witch when she'd been vulnerable to evil. An ancient agreement between good and evil allowed two days for a new witch to choose sides. In Paige's case, The Source had attempted to trick her into joining the side of evil.

Paige wondered if something like that could be going on with Lily. Maybe an agent of evil had somehow tricked them all into thinking that Lily hadn't received her powers. That way, evil could take advantage of this time to lure the teen to the dark side. *I should do a spell to reveal any other magic that's currently working on Lily,* Paige thought. First, though, she wanted to make sure she knew everything about Lily's missing magic.

"Was there a ceremony or anything?" Paige asked.

"Kind of," Lily replied. "Mom made me wear this old nightgown thing and recite a spell."

Paige wrinkled her nose. "An old nightgown?"

"It used to be a dress. It's been handed down in my family for a long time. It's one of the only things we have left. I guess all the other witches wore it when they received their powers."

"What about the spell?" Paige asked. "Did your mom write it down for you?"

"Are you kidding?" Lily said. "We're not allowed to write anything down. I started memorizing that spell when I was five. Mom wanted to make sure I could become a witch even if something happened to her."

Paige nodded. Juliana had certainly done her best to prepare Lily for the future. "Can you tell me the words?" she asked.

Lily nodded and began to recite:

> *I call upon you, elements four.*
> *Unlock your secrets forevermore.*
> *A new witch enters the fold.*
> *Allow her magic to take hold.*

Paige half expected to feel a magic wind blow through the room, endowing Lily with her missing powers. But nothing happened. Lily sighed. "That's pretty much the way it went yesterday," she said.

"Is that the same spell your mom used to receive her powers?" Paige asked. Lily nodded. "Then I guess she's pretty sure she got the words right," Paige murmured.

Lily plopped down on the floor. "Can I call Drew?" she asked.

"No," Paige said. "Piper is making sure she's okay, remember?" She studied the girl. Why was she so worried about Drew all the time? Paige thought back to when she had become a Charmed One. During the magical forty-eight-hour window when she could choose good or evil, The Source had taken on the form of her current boyfriend and used her trust in him to lead her toward evildoing. It was possible that some evil creature was using Lily's friendship with Drew the same way.

"Didn't you tell me Drew was there when you were supposed to get your powers?" Paige asked.

Lily nodded. "She was in my room. My mom and I were in the living room."

"Why wasn't Drew at school?" Paige asked.

"I dunno," Lily said. "She didn't feel like going." Lily avoided Paige's eyes as she said this.

"You mean she was skipping school?" Paige pressed. "And your mom didn't mind?"

Lily didn't answer. Paige studied her. She'd had a feeling all day that Lily was lying to her about Drew. But she also had a feeling that Lily might be ready to tell the truth now.

"Lily," Paige said. "Your mother didn't know Drew was there yesterday, did she?"

"No," Lily mumbled. "But she wouldn't have cared. Drew's there all the time."

"I think your mother would have cared if she knew Drew was cutting school and hiding in your bedroom while you were performing a magical rite," Paige said. "I think she would have cared a lot."

"I guess," Lily said.

"Your mom says she swore you to silence about the fact that you two are witches," Paige said. "But I have a feeling that you told Drew anyway."

Lily nodded without looking up.

Paige sat down cross-legged on the floor across from Lily. It was time to level with the girl. In her social work Paige had discovered that kids didn't like it when adults talked down to them as if they were babies. They appreciated it when adults treated them as equals, and that's what Paige planned to do.

"Listen, we're getting somewhere now," Paige said, looking Lily in the eye. "I have a theory about what's going on. I'm not sure it's right, but I'm gonna need you to be really honest with me so that I can figure it out. Okay?"

Lily nodded.

"How long have you been friends with Drew?" Paige asked.

"Since we were six," Lily said. "We were reading partners in first grade."

It's hard to believe Drew was a six-year-old demon, Paige thought. *Maybe whatever evil is influencing her only took over when it was time for Lily to get her powers.*

"Has Drew been acting strange lately?" Paige asked. "In the last day or two, I mean?"

Lily's green eyes widened, but she clamped her mouth shut.

I'll take that as a yes, Paige thought. "Lily, you have to be honest with me, remember?" she said aloud.

"I promised Drew I wouldn't tell anyone," Lily said.

"This is important," Paige told her seriously. "No one is going to be mad at Drew. But we need to keep you safe, and without your powers you aren't safe. Now tell me, how has Drew been different lately?"

"It's like she's under a spell," Lily whispered. "Weird things keep happening."

"Weird how?" Paige asked.

"Like when her hair turned blue," Lily said. "We were just sitting in her room yesterday and it turned blue. That's when her mom freaked out."

Paige frowned, confused. "Wait a minute, I thought Drew was at *your* house yesterday," she said.

"She was. But after my powers didn't show up, I was supposed to just wait in my room and clear my mind to make myself a better receptacle."

Paige suppressed a smile at Lily's sarcastic tone of voice. "You mean you were supposed to meditate or something?"

"Yeah," Lily said. "But it was stupid, so Drew said we should sneak out and go hang at her place."

Paige raised her eyebrows. "Do you two sneak around a lot?" she asked.

"Kinda," Lily said. "My mom's really over-protective."

"Okay, so you went over to Drew's," Paige said. "And what happened when her hair turned blue?"

"Nothing," Lily said. "We were just sitting there, and Drew said she liked my sweater, which is blue. And then her hair turned that same color."

"Did you feel any power in the air when her hair changed?" Paige asked. "Do you remember thinking anything about her hair, or wanting to change her hair?"

"You think *I* did it?" Lily snorted. "I didn't do anything. I have no powers, remember?"

Paige thought about it. Obviously Drew either had powers of her own, or else she was using Lily's powers without Lily knowing. But how would that help her convince Lily to choose the side of evil?

"You and Drew both keep running away today," she said. "Do you do that a lot?"

"No!" Lily sounded offended. "I was just trying to help Drew."

"But Drew's parents said she's a juvenile delinquent," Paige said. "So Drew must be in trouble a lot, right?"

Lily looked at her hands. "She didn't used to be," she said. "But for the past year she's been running away a lot, and she shoplifts sometimes. And once I saw her smoking, but I don't think she really liked it." She gazed up at Paige defiantly. "But it's her parents' fault. They always treat her like she's bad even when she isn't. They're crazy."

Paige thought Lily was probably right about the influence Drew's parents had on her wild behavior. Unfortunately that might not be the only problem with Drew.

"Lily, do you think Drew's behavior has changed since you said the spell to receive your powers?" she asked. "Has she gotten worse at all?"

"I guess. . . ." Lily looked confused. "It's been weirder. Like the hair thing."

"And since then, Drew has convinced you to do the kinds of things she does," Paige said. "Like running away and stealing things."

Lily nodded sheepishly.

"That's what I was afraid of." Paige sighed. It was bad enough when demons got adults involved with their nefarious plans. But to use an innocent girl like Drew to get at Lily—that was true evil!

"What do you think is going on?" Lily asked.

"The forces of evil are using Drew to convince you to misbehave," Paige said. "If you do it enough, you'll be corrupted. You'll choose to be an evil witch rather than a good one."

"But I'm not even a witch yet," Lily protested.

"I think you are," Paige said. "But an evil creature has convinced you that your powers don't work."

"You mean Gortag?" Lily asked.

"No," Paige said. "I mean Drew."

Drew watched from under the bed as Piper paced around the bedroom. "Leo!" Piper yelled. "Leo! I need you!"

But Leo didn't appear in that white light the way Drew had seen him do earlier. What did Lily say they called it? Orbing.

These people have some freaky powers, Drew thought.

Piper plopped down on the bed with a frustrated sigh. Drew couldn't blame her. It was no fun being trapped in the bedroom. Her parents locked *her* in here often enough, whenever she behaved in a way they didn't like—which was often. She crept forward until she was peering out from under the hem of her dark purple sheet, which hung off the bed haphazardly as usual. Drew never made her bed.

All she could see of Piper now were her feet. Drew twitched her nose as she studied the witch's chocolate-brown boots. She wasn't sure whether or not to let Piper know she was here. The Halliwells' job was to protect Lily. So why had one of them come looking for *her*? Did Piper know what was really going on?

Drew crept forward a little more, and as she did her foot scraped against a notebook that she'd shoved under the bed. Surprised, Drew jumped away from it. She froze immediately, hoping Piper hadn't heard her.

No such luck. Piper got off the bed and knelt on the floor two inches away from Drew. She pulled up the sheet, peered into the darkness under the bed, and gasped.

• • •

Piper stared at the mouse under Drew's bed. It looked right back at her, unmoving. "That's it," she muttered. "These people are definitely unfit parents."

Drew's room was a mess—dirty clothes strewn all over the floor, the sheets hanging half off the bed. The dust on the desk was so thick that Drew had managed to write her name in it the way you would write in sand with a finger. Clearly Mrs. Elson never cleaned in here.

Piper dropped the sheet and stood. She had to get out of here. It was no good trying to force the door open—she'd already given herself a blister on one finger twisting the doorknob. The lock was strong. *I guess when you have a kid who keeps running away, you need a strong lock to keep her in,* she thought. It was just one more example of how the Elsons needed parenting training. Piper scanned the filthy room, looking for anything that would help her get out or contact her sisters.

"Leo!" she called again. Nothing happened.

Her husband wasn't answering. Usually he came as soon as she called him, the way he orbed to any witch in his charge who was having trouble. But she'd been yelling his name for ten minutes and he still wasn't here. Piper tried to push down the frightened thoughts that rose in her mind. Leo would never willingly leave her in a bad situation. Not unless he was in some kind of trouble himself.

Piper crossed to the window and peered

outside, taking in the long drop to the sidewalk. "I wish I could orb," she muttered. A strangled scream behind her made her jump. Piper whirled around, hands raised to freeze or explode.

"Don't!" cried Drew, cowering. Piper dropped her hands to her sides, astonished. Drew was lying half under the bed, with only her head and shoulders sticking out.

"Where did you come from?" Piper cried.

"I was hiding," Drew mumbled.

Piper went over and pulled Drew from under the bed, helping her to her feet. "You were hiding under the bed?" Piper asked.

Drew nodded, not meeting her eyes.

Piper raised an eyebrow. "That's interesting," she said. "Because I looked under that bed about thirty seconds ago, and you weren't there."

"I was too," Drew argued. "You just didn't see me."

"Oh, please," Piper said. "It's a twin bed—I would've seen you if you were there. The only thing under that bed was a mouse." The words were out of Piper's mouth before their meaning sunk in. Drew's strange disappearance . . . the mouse under the bed . . . the strange little scream a minute ago . . .

Drew ran to the bed and leaped under the covers to hide. Piper grabbed the blanket and yanked it back off the girl.

"*You* were the mouse," Piper said. "You turned yourself into a mouse and back."

"No, I didn't," Drew insisted.

"That's how you vanished during the fight outside the library," Piper went on, thinking aloud. "You turned into a mouse there and no one saw you run away."

"A squirrel," Drew said, defeated. "I turned into a squirrel. And then by the time it wore off, you had all orbed away again. I didn't know where to go, so I came home."

"But your parents don't know you're here," Piper said.

Drew shrugged. "I turned into a mouse before I came into the apartment. They didn't see me."

"How are you doing all this?" Piper asked, an accusing tone creeping into her voice.

"Dunno."

"Why did you turn back into yourself just now?"

"I wasn't expecting to. It just happened." Drew faked a yawn as if she were bored, but Piper could tell the girl was covering her true feelings. Drew was afraid.

Piper sat down next to her on the bed. "What if I tell you I've met people before who could turn into animals?" she said. "My own sister turned into a dog once."

Drew stared at her, wide-eyed, but said nothing.

"It's true," Piper went on. "Does that make you feel better?"

Drew put her angry face back on. "No, it

makes me think you're nuts," she snapped. But her voice trembled. Piper stared at Drew until the teen met her eye.

"Drew, how long has this been going on?" she asked.

"Since yesterday," Drew mumbled.

Yesterday? *Lily's birthday*, Piper thought. That seemed like a strange coincidence. "And what exactly is happening?" she asked Drew.

"First my hair turned blue," Drew said. "Then this morning I turned into a squirrel."

A smile twitched at Piper's lips. "Just like that?"

"Yeah." Drew noticed Piper's expression and slowly smiled back. "I sound like a freak."

"No," Piper said. "You sound like a witch."

Drew's face paled. "What do you mean?" she said quickly. "There's no such thing as witches."

"That's not true," Piper said. "I'm a witch."

Drew gasped and drew back, but Piper was finally beginning to get the hang of this dealing-with-kids thing. She could tell that Drew was faking her surprise. "And Lily is a witch," she added. "But you knew that already, didn't you?"

"No!" Drew turned her face away.

"You and Lily are best friends," Piper pressed. "Did she tell you about her family? About how they're all witches who receive their powers when they turn thirteen?"

Drew didn't answer.

"Come on, Drew, I know what's going on,"

Piper said, although that was only half true. "These things that are happening to you—that's why Lily keeps running away. She's trying to help you figure out what's going on."

"Lily's mother has been teaching her all about being a witch for years," Drew whispered. "She should know how to deal with this stuff."

"When did Lily tell you she was a witch?"

Drew laughed. "When we were like eight. She was trying to scare me."

Piper couldn't believe it. All these years, Juliana had assumed Lily was keeping their secret. But of course a little girl wouldn't understand the need for such strict secrecy. Of course a little girl would tell her best friend. And who knows how many other people had found out the O'Farrells' secret since then? *Forget about Gortag*, Piper thought. *There could be hundreds of other evil things out there who knew there would be some good witch hunting yesterday.* On the day a witch was to receive her powers, there was a moment when the powers existed unprotected in space, a moment before the powers found the witch who called for them. It might only last a split second, but if an evil creature knew when it was going to happen, it could wreak havoc trying to steal the powers, kill the new witch, or both. Piper sighed. This was worse than they'd thought.

"Drew, what time did your hair turn blue yesterday?" she asked.

"In the afternoon," Drew said.

"Do you remember what happened just before it changed color?"

Drew nodded. "Me and Lily were in my room and I was looking at her sweater. I remember thinking I liked the color. Then my hair turned that color."

"Were you touching your hair?"

"Maybe," Drew said. "I can't really remember."

"So you and Lily were both in here?" Piper got up and began looking around the room.

"Yeah," said Drew. "We came over here after her initiation thing didn't work."

"Her what?"

"You know, the thing where she called for her powers. It totally didn't work. Then we hung out for a while in her room waiting for some magic. But nothing happened, and she was really freaking out. So I said we should come over here. I thought it would distract her."

"It sounds like you saw her initiation spell firsthand," Piper commented.

"Yeah, I was hiding in her room," Drew said. "Her mom doesn't know I know they're witches. So I had to pretend I didn't know about it."

"Why were you there if you weren't supposed to know about it?" Piper asked.

Drew rolled her eyes. "Are you kidding? She was getting magic powers! It was the coolest thing that ever happened. I mean, it was supposed to be." She blew a strand of blue hair out of her eyes. "It's not so cool now."

Piper was deep in thought as she listened. So Drew had been in the house when Lily was calling for her powers. Was it possible that the powers had attached themselves to the wrong girl? It would explain why none of them had felt any power attached to Lily, and why Leo had only been able to sense Lily today when she was with Drew.

"We have to get to the Manor," she said.

"Why?" Drew asked.

"Because I think you somehow ended up with Lily's powers," Piper explained. "And if you're not meant to have powers, they might be too much for you to handle. Meanwhile, Lily's enemies know she's a witch, but she's unprotected."

"You mean they're gonna keep coming after her?" Drew asked, frowning.

"Yes," Piper said. "And they'll think she has powers to protect herself, but she doesn't."

"Because I have them." A big tear made its way down Drew's cheek. "I didn't mean to take them."

Piper studied her face. This girl had been a brat all day, but something made Piper believe her. "I know you didn't mean to," she said gently. "But we still have to fix this."

She looked back at the locked door. "Unfortunately I don't know how we're going to get out of here without making a mess. But your parents are just gonna have to deal with that."

She waved her hands to explode the door. The peeling paint on the door exploded off in small burning scraps, but the door stayed intact. Piper stared at it in surprise. Drew stamped out the burning paint chunks.

"What's going on?" Drew asked.

Piper wasn't sure how to answer. It seemed as if the room was magic-resistant somehow. She couldn't explode the door, and she couldn't get through to Leo. Plus, Drew had said she was a mouse when she came in, but then her shape-shifting spell had just reversed itself without warning. It was as if someone was trying to keep Drew's magic contained in this room. But that was impossible . . . unless someone else knew that Drew was the one who had Lily's powers.

She thought briefly of Drew's parents. They *had* locked her in here. "Do your parents know about the O'Farrells?" she asked Drew. "That they're witches?"

Drew snorted. "They'd ship me off to an asylum if I started talking about witches. Besides, I don't want to get Ms. O'Farrell in trouble. She's nicer to me than my own parents."

"And they didn't suspect anything . . . magical . . . when your hair turned blue?"

"No way," Drew said. "They've barely even spoken to me since then."

"So they don't know about you turning into squirrels or mice?"

Drew shook her head. "And I can't let them find out," she added. "I'm not kidding, they really will send me to military school or something."

Piper couldn't help but agree. The Elsons were pretty extreme, and they didn't seem especially fond of their daughter. *She might be better off away at school,* Piper thought sadly. The more time she spent with Drew, the more sympathy she had for the girl. It seemed as if the only good thing in Drew's life was her friendship with Lily.

But there were more immediate worries than Drew's family situation. They had to figure out who could've turned the girl's room into a magical no-fly zone.

"Drew, you saw that demon at the library, right?" Piper asked.

"The one who looked like a devil?" Drew replied.

"Yup. Gortag."

Drew nodded. "From the way Lily's mom always described Gortag, I thought he'd be like ten feet tall and have fangs or something."

"Yeah, well, he's plenty dangerous the way he is," Piper told her. "Have you ever seen him before?"

"No. I didn't even really believe in demons until today. I thought all those demon stories were like ghost stories for witches."

"I'll tell you a few real ghost stories some-time," Piper said wryly. "But for now we have to figure out if Gortag put some kind of spell on you."

"You mean I might have gotten Lily's powers because Gortag messed up her initiation spell?"

"No, I was thinking more like Gortag saw the two of you together at the library. He was able to sense the O'Farrell powers in you, so he put a binding spell on you or something. To keep you trapped in this room."

Drew blushed.

"What?" Piper asked.

"Well . . . I'm not trapped," Drew pointed out. "*You* are. Sorry."

"You mean because you can just turn back into a mouse?" Piper asked, confused.

"No. I can't do that on command. It just happens," Drew said. "But I can just yell for my parents to let me out."

"They don't even know you're home," Piper argued.

"Yeah, but that would make them come even faster," Drew said. "They'd want to know where I was hiding all this time."

"That's perfect!" Piper cried. "Do you think they'll open the door? Even though they know I'm in here?"

"Maybe," Drew said. "They might want to yell at me right to my face. And they're probably not afraid of you."

"If they open the door, I'm going to try to freeze them," Piper told her. "It won't hurt them—it just stops time for them for a little while, and then we can get past them and out the front door. Will you be okay if I do that?"

"Will they see us while they're frozen?"

"Nope," Piper assured her.

"And then we'll go to your house and you'll fix the power mix-up?"

"It might take a while to figure out just how you ended up with Lily's powers, but I promise that eventually it will all make sense."

"Okay." Drew went over to the door and took a deep breath. "Mom!" she bellowed. "Dad!"

Piper positioned herself at the side of the door, ready to freeze the Elsons the instant the door opened. She heard loud footsteps echoing down the hallway. "Drew? What are you doing here?" Mr. Elson bellowed.

"I was hiding under the bed," Drew called back.

"Is that . . . that woman still in there?" Mrs. Elson asked. She was right on the other side of the door. "Tell her we called the police."

"What!" Piper cried, unable to stop herself. "Why?"

"You've been harassing us all day," Mr. Elson growled. "Drew, you'll just have to wait."

This wasn't going according to plan at all. Piper shot Drew a panicked look. "Say you need the restroom," she whispered.

"But I have to use the bathroom," Drew whined.

There was a mumbled conversation outside the door. "Too bad," Mr. Elson finally said. Piper could hardly believe her ears. How could these people be so mean to their own child?

"When the police get here, I'll be sure to tell them how you treat Drew," Piper called in what she hoped was a threatening tone.

Another mumbled conversation outside was followed by the sound of the lock turning. Drew grinned in triumph, and Piper was shocked by the way a simple smile transformed the girl's face. Drew had been wearing a perma-scowl all day; it hadn't even occurred to Piper that she *could* smile.

The doorknob began to turn. "Get ready," Piper whispered. Drew nodded. As soon as the door opened an inch, Drew threw all her weight against it. The door quickly swung outward, wide enough for Piper to catch a glimpse of the Elsons standing on the other side. She froze them immediately.

"Let's go," she told Drew, hurrying out of the prisonlike room. She started down the hallway toward the living room, assuming that Drew was right on her heels. When she turned back, though, she saw Drew still in the doorway to her bedroom. The girl was rooted in place, staring at her parents.

Mr. Elson was frozen with his mouth open in

the beginnings of an angry yell. His wife was frozen holding her hands up as if to strike or push whoever came through the door. Drew studied them in astonishment. Piper gave her a moment—all this new information about witches and demons and magical powers was a lot for a young girl to take in. She'd forgotten that Drew might be startled by seeing people actually frozen in time.

"We have to go," Piper told her. "The freeze will wear off soon."

"Can't you just refreeze them?" Drew asked.

"Well . . . yes," Piper said. "But that wouldn't be nice. They aren't *evil* people."

Drew snorted. "That's not what I think," she muttered. But she turned and followed Piper to the living room and out the front door.

"Leo!" Piper called. This time her husband answered. White light filled the dingy hallway, and Leo appeared with a worried face.

"Piper! What—"

"No time for questions," Piper said, shoving Drew toward Leo. "We have to go before her parents unfreeze."

Leo grabbed Piper's hand, took hold of Drew's arm, and orbed them home.

Chapter

8

Phoebe chewed on the end of her pencil. She sat curled in the corner of the living room sofa, working on the spell to vanquish Gortag. Juliana sat on the other end of the sofa, looking through a Halliwell family photo album.

"It must be nice to live in a house that's been in your family for so many generations," she commented, looking at a picture of Grams as a young woman in front of the Manor.

Phoebe smiled. "I guess. I didn't always appreciate it."

"You should," Juliana said. "Family history matters."

Phoebe knew she was thinking of her brother and all the others Gortag had killed over the years. "I'm sorry we alerted Gortag to your hiding place," Phoebe said softly. "We're only trying to help, but I know we ruined the only place you felt safe, your home."

Juliana's eyes took on a faraway look. "I never really felt safe there," she said. "I've never felt safe anywhere. My clan was always on the move—we were travelers."

"Like gypsies?" Phoebe asked.

"Sort of. Irish travelers. We lived like gypsies, but we don't share the same heritage. And in our case, we were always on the move so we could stay ahead of Gortag. He would always find us, always kill one or two family members before we could escape."

"That's awful," Phoebe said. She and her sisters were frequently the target of demons and various forces of evil. But she couldn't imagine how it would feel to lose so many family members to the same demon. "You must really hate Gortag," she commented.

"I'm afraid of him," Juliana admitted. "My whole clan lived in fear of him for generations. I don't think it occurred to anyone that we should try to vanquish him. It's like they all accepted the fact that he would forever be hunting us. I don't want that for Lily. I want her to grow up feeling strong, not being scared all the time."

"We'll help you get that for her," Phoebe said. "I'm almost done with the vanquishing spell."

Juliana sat up straight, her eyes hopeful. "Will it work?"

"Well . . ." Phoebe glanced down at the words scribbled on her journal page. "I'm sure this spell will bind him into one body, but I'm not entirely certain that it will also vanquish him."

"Maybe we have to do that in a separate spell," Juliana suggested. "One to bind him, another to vanquish him once he's bound."

"It's an idea," Phoebe agreed. She was just about to get started on another spell when Leo orbed in with Piper and a blue-haired teen that Phoebe assumed was Drew. As soon as the white light faded, Drew turned to Leo, eyes shining.

"That was so cool!" she cried. "I could feel all my molecules buzzing around."

Leo grinned.

"It felt kinda like that when I turned into a mouse. What did you call it?" she asked, turning to Piper.

"Shapeshifting."

"It felt like that when I shapeshifted," Drew went on, talking to Leo. "All tingly. But then it stopped when I became the mouse and the squirrel."

"Don't get too used to the magic, missy," Piper told her. "It's only borrowed."

"I know," Drew said. "And it was a little scary too. Orbing was way more fun."

Phoebe had no idea what they were talking about. Still, it was hard not to enjoy Drew's enthusiasm . . . until she caught sight of Juliana's face. The woman had gone white, and she was digging her fingernails into the arm of the sofa. Phoebe's mind immediately returned to the problem at hand—and that was Lily, not Drew. "Um, hello?" she said, waving to Piper and Leo. "What are you talking about?"

All three of them turned to her. "Are you Phoebe?" Drew asked. "I didn't meet you yet."

Juliana leaped up off the couch, in no mood for small talk. "What is going on?" she demanded. "Did you say that Drew *shapeshifted*?"

Phoebe had the same question. "Do we have *two* witches on our hands?" she asked.

Piper shook her head. "No, but I think we've found Lily's missing powers," she said. "Drew got them."

Juliana's eyes widened. She stepped closer to Drew and brushed a strand of dark blue hair off her forehead. "Is that what this is all about?" she asked gently.

Drew nodded. "I don't know how it happened," she said.

"And the shapeshifting?" Juliana asked.

"I turned into a squirrel, and then a mouse," Drew replied, excitement creeping back into her voice. "At first it was kinda scary, 'cause I didn't know what was happening. But then when I figured it out, it was so cool. I ran straight up a tree trunk."

Juliana smiled indulgently. "Sounds like fun,"

she said. Her voice was affectionate, but her eyes were worried. Phoebe admired the woman's kindness. Here she was, scared sick about her daughter's missing magic and the demon that was hunting them both, but she was taking the time to chat with Drew about her shapeshifting. Clearly she felt a bond with Lily's friend. But that still didn't explain how Drew had gotten involved in this situation.

"Someone want to fill me in?" Phoebe asked.

"I found Drew under her bed looking just like any other scared little mouse," Piper said. "Then all of a sudden she was herself again." She turned to Juliana. "These weird things began happening to her yesterday at your house after Lily recited the spell to activate her powers."

"At *my* house?" Juliana repeated. "But Drew wasn't there."

All eyes turned to Drew. She blushed. "I was in Lily's room," she admitted.

Juliana stared at her, shocked. "Did you hear what we were doing?"

Drew nodded.

"She's known all along that you were witches," Piper said.

Juliana's mouth dropped open. "How?" she cried.

"Lily told me," Drew said. "But she made me promise not to tell! And I never told anyone, ever. Don't be mad at us."

Juliana sank down onto the couch. "I'm not mad," she said. "I'm just . . . surprised. I can't believe Lily's been lying to me all this time."

Phoebe sat down next to her, thinking back to a developmental psych class she took in college. "Sometimes it's hard to remember that kids have their own lives and can make their own decisions," she said. "You've been so busy hiding Lily from Gortag and training her in the craft that you may not have noticed that she's also just a regular kid. Girls tell secrets to their best friends."

"I guess they do," Juliana said, looking at Drew. "Is that why you were at our house yesterday?" she asked the girl. "Did you know Lily was going to get her powers?"

"Yeah," Drew said. "I was psyched for her. I wanted to be there to see what power she got."

Phoebe tried to stay focused on the problem at hand. "So the question is, how did Drew end up with Lily's powers?"

"I think she stole them," said a voice from behind her.

Surprised, Phoebe glanced over her shoulder to see Paige, with Lily, enter the living room. Paige's expression was deadly serious, and she stared at Drew intensely. Phoebe had never seen her sister look so angry.

"Whoa, Paige, what do you mean?" Phoebe asked.

Paige ignored her and addressed Drew

instead. "Who are you really?" she demanded. "Who sent you?"

"Paige!" Phoebe jumped up and grabbed her younger sister's arm. "What are you doing?"

"Do you remember when I first became a Charmed One?" Paige asked her.

"Of course," Phoebe said. "You started orbing around without knowing what was going on."

"And you freaked out about it," Piper added dryly.

"That's not what I mean," Paige said. "There was a mystical forty-eight-hour rule."

"An ancient agreement between good and evil," Leo put in. "During which time you could decide whether to use your powers to help others or to help yourself. Good or evil."

"Right," Paige said. "You guys were trying to convince me that being a witch meant I could do good in the world. But the evil side wasn't playing fair."

"What are you talking about?" Juliana demanded. She had her arm protectively around Drew's shoulders.

"The Source took over my boyfriend's body," Paige began.

"What source?" Juliana asked.

"The Source of all evil," Phoebe explained. "Boy, I could tell you stories about him—"

"Anyway," Paige interrupted. "The Source used someone I trusted to try to convince me that I should turn toward the evil side—by asking for my help to save an innocent. But it would've meant killing someone in order to save the innocent. It would've meant becoming a murderer. Evil."

"And you're saying that something evil is using Drew the same way?" Phoebe asked, confused.

Paige nodded. "Yes. To trick Lily into joining the side of evil." She turned to Lily, who stood next to her, brow knit with worry. "Hasn't Drew been asking you for help all day?"

"Yes," Lily whispered. "She wanted me to help her figure out why her hair turned blue and make it go back to normal."

"Isn't she the one who told you to steal the Book of Shadows?" Paige pressed.

"Kind of," Lily said.

"See what I mean?" Paige cried. "She's acting just like Shane did when I first received *my* powers."

Phoebe had forgotten about that magical forty-eight-hour grace period. She knew what a close call it had been for Paige. Still, she wasn't convinced that the same thing was happening to Lily. "But it's not the same situation," she said aloud. "You *had* powers, so The Source tried to turn you evil. Lily doesn't have powers yet."

"Besides, if Drew stole Lily's powers, and Drew was evil, she'd just kill Lily," Piper pointed out. "Why bother sticking around to trick her into anything?"

"What if she didn't really steal Lily's powers?" Paige argued. "What if she's just tricking us all into thinking Lily is powerless?"

"We did a magic-reveal spell," Piper said. "Twice."

"Maybe she did a counterspell," Paige replied.

"No!" Drew said emphatically. "I don't even know what you're talking about! Lily's the witch, not me. I didn't steal her powers. I just wanted her to help me get rid of them. That's why I wanted your book." She looked beseechingly at her best friend. "Tell them, Lil."

"I told her that you had a book with all kinds of spells," Lily agreed. "Drew thought there might be a spell to reverse whatever magic turned her hair blue."

"That's what she told you," Paige said. "But she could've been lying, trying to get you to do bad things like running away and stealing our book." Paige glanced at Juliana, who was still standing with Drew. "All day long Lily has been complaining about you, about how much pressure she's under to get her powers."

"What?" Juliana cried.

"Shut up!" Lily yelled at the same time. "I didn't say you could tell my mother that!"

"Lily, don't be so rude," Juliana said automatically.

"Don't tell me what to do!" Lily snapped.

Phoebe couldn't believe it—her sister had started a full-scale family feud! "Paige, this isn't helping," Phoebe told her.

"All I meant to say was that Lily is already in a negative head space," Paige said, trying to smooth things over. "And therefore, she's vulnerable to evil influences."

"I'm not an evil influence," Drew put in, her voice trembling. "I didn't do anything wrong."

"You're always doing bad things!" Lily retorted. "Your own parents think you're a brat."

"My parents are jerks!" Drew cried. "I can't believe you're taking their side!"

"Well, you stole my powers," Lily said.

"I did not!"

Phoebe wasn't sure whom to believe. Piper and Leo looked just as confused as she felt, and poor Juliana stood with her mouth hanging open, speechless, as the girls fought.

"You've always been jealous of me," Lily told Drew.

"I have not!" Drew replied.

"You're jealous because my mother is cool and yours is weird," Lily said. "And you're jealous because I'm a witch."

"You wish!" Drew cried, her face red with anger. "What kind of witch are you? You don't even have any powers. I do."

"That's because you *stole* them," Lily yelled, just as mad. "Thief!"

All of a sudden, Drew's blue hair turned a

tawny yellow color at the roots. Before Phoebe
knew what was happening, the yellowish color
moved down to the ends of Drew's hair. Then
the hair grew over her face, spreading down her
neck to her arms, which lengthened until they
formed two front legs ending in massive paws
with razor-sharp claws. Meanwhile her entire
body had become covered by the tawny hair.
Her green eyes lightened to a speckled-gold
color, and her face grew flat and wide. As the
transformation became complete, Drew opened
her mouth and roared, revealing a mouth full of
long, deadly teeth.

"She's a lion!" Juliana gasped.

"She's a pissed-off lion," Phoebe replied.

Drew gathered herself into a crouch, her
supple muscles bunched to spring at Lily. With
a snarl she launched herself into the air.

Piper waved her hands to freeze Drew in
mid-jump.

Phoebe was so awestruck by the savage—and
beautiful—creature that Drew had become that
it took her a moment to realize what had happened. Lily knelt on the rug, frozen while ducking from Drew's attack. Meanwhile, Drew had
leaped right over her, completely unfrozen.

With a roar of frustration, Drew turned back
to pounce again.

"She won't freeze!" Piper cried in a panic. She
waved her hands, unfreezing Lily.

At lightning speed Phoebe reached out and

grabbed Lily by the arm, yanking her out of the path of the charging lioness. Drew the lion whirled around and ran at them again.

"Help!" Lily screamed. Phoebe shoved the girl behind her and dropped into a fighting stance. But all the martial arts training in the world wasn't going to help her stop a wild animal of such strength. She prepared for the impact of Drew's charge.

"Stop it," Juliana said loudly, stepping right in front of the lion. *"Now."*

The lion was in mid-leap with its claws out and fangs bared when it saw Juliana. Phoebe saw an expression of human horror pass through its golden eyes. The lion retracted its claws, pulled its front legs in to its chest, and tumbled to the ground at Juliana's feet. It looked as embarrassed as a house cat caught falling down while someone was watching. But it stayed put, gazing up at Juliana apologetically.

Phoebe's heart was still pounding furiously. She'd never been so terrified by anything as she'd been by seeing the bloodlust in the eyes of that huge cat as it attacked. She could hardly believe that Juliana had been brave enough to simply step in front of it.

"Drew, come back," Juliana said, bending to stroke the giant cat's furry head. "Just calm down and come back to us."

The lion ducked its head, fur darkening at its

ears. Quickly the fur turned to dark brown hair. Drew's skin returned to normal, her front legs shortened into arms, and her tail disappeared. She was herself again, sitting on the floor in front of Juliana. For a moment nobody spoke. They were all too shaken up.

"At least your hair isn't blue anymore," Phoebe joked, trying to break the tension.

Drew pulled a lock of hair in front of her and looked at it. Then her eyes filled with tears and she began to sob. "What's wrong with me?" she cried. "I didn't mean to do that! I was mad, but I didn't want to hurt anyone! I didn't do it on purpose."

"I know," Juliana said, helping the sobbing girl up. "I believe you."

Paige hurried forward to settle Drew on the couch. "I believe you too," she said. "I'm sorry I said you were evil."

Phoebe heard a sniffle from behind her and turned to see that Lily had begun crying as well. "Um, Juliana?" she said.

Juliana noticed her daughter's tears and rushed over to give her a hug. "Oh, honey, I'm so sorry. You must've been terrified!"

Lily nodded.

"I'm sorry, Lil," Drew said from the couch.

"No, you're not," Lily said through her tears. "You were gonna attack me, but you didn't want to hurt my mother. You care more about her than me!"

"I was so mad at you. . . ." Drew's voice trailed off as Lily continued to sob.

Phoebe sat next to her, letting Juliana comfort Lily. "Drew, do you remember what happened right before you changed shape?" she asked. "Did you wish you could be a lion?"

"No," Drew mumbled. "I just wanted to be strong so I could attack Lily. She was saying mean things and I wanted to defend myself. But I didn't want to turn into a lion and kill her!"

Phoebe exchanged a look with Paige over Drew's head. "That seems emotional, but not evil," Phoebe commented.

"The first time Drew shapeshifted it was because she wanted to get away from her parents without being seen," Piper put in. "It seems like the powers are responding to her emotions. She's not thinking that she wants to be this animal or that animal. Her body just knows how to turn into whatever animal best suits her emotional needs at that moment."

"I don't know how to control it," Drew said. "Lily had all that training—she's supposed to be the one doing all this. You would know how to handle it, Lil."

Lily had stopped crying. Now she just looked frightened. "No," she said. "I don't want that power. That's too much." She glanced up at her mother. "If that's my power, I don't want it!"

"But Drew's right, Lily," Phoebe said. "You've been preparing for witch-hood your whole life.

You could probably control the shapeshifting better than Drew."

"I don't care," Lily said. "I don't want to do that. It's too scary."

Phoebe felt helpless. If Drew had ended up with Lily's powers, they had to be given back. But how?

Chapter
9

"Are you sure this is going to work?" Juliana asked nervously.

Piper looked around at all the preparations in the attic—two separate protective circles were marked on the floor with white silk cords. The area in between the circles had been cleared, and Leo was sweeping the wooden floor with a brush made of sage. Piper took a deep breath. "No," she said. "I'm not sure."

She watched as Juliana's face fell. Piper hated to upset the woman, but she had to tell her the truth. The Book of Shadows said that a transfer-of-powers spell would only work if the two witches were equals, and if both wanted the powers transferred. But their two witches— Drew and Lily—weren't equals at all, and at the moment Lily didn't really want the powers. It didn't look good for the spell.

"The Book of Shadows has a way of giving us the information we need when we need it," Piper told Juliana. "And when I came up here, it was open to this spell. That means it's our best chance to get Lily's powers back where they belong."

"Our best chance?" Juliana said skeptically.

"But not necessarily a *good* chance," Leo put in.

"We have to do what we can to make sure all the conditions are right for the spell to work," Piper said. "There's no way we can make both Drew and Lily equal witches—"

"Then what's the use?" Juliana interrupted.

Piper told herself to stay calm. Juliana's tone was sharp, but Piper knew it was because she was worried. She was used to handling everything on her own, and she still wasn't used to trusting the Charmed Ones, or Leo.

"I'm hoping that since Lily is a hereditary witch with the inherent ability to handle magic, and Drew has magical powers at the moment, they'll count as being equal right now," Piper explained.

"I think that makes sense," Leo said. He handed the sage broom to Piper. "I've cleared the space for the mediator," he told her.

Piper checked out the clean-swept area in the middle of the floor. If the spell worked as it should, both Lily and Drew would stand in their protective circles while a mediator from Lily's family occupied the space in between them. The mediator—presumably an ancestor witch of the O'Farrells—would decide whether or not to transfer the powers from Drew to Lily.

"Right before we start, we have to put a bowl of water in the center of the cleared space," Piper said. "But other than that, I guess we're all set up."

"Before you get started, I want to check in with the Elders," Leo said. "Just in case there's an easier way to put Lily's magic back in the right girl."

"They won't help us," Juliana said dully.

"They won't help *you*," Leo agreed, "because you turned your back on them. Do you want to change your mind?"

She stared at him for a long beat. "No," she said finally. "They should have put a stop to Gortag's carnage a hundred years ago."

"I'm sorry," Leo said. "The Elders are not all-powerful. I'm sorry they couldn't help. But they may be willing to help Lily even if they can't help you."

"Good idea," Piper said. "I don't think we're emotionally ready to start for a little while anyway. Why don't you go ask."

Leo nodded and orbed out.

"What did you mean by that?" Juliana asked, her face pinched with anxiety. "Why aren't we emotionally ready?"

"The other requirement for the transfer spell to work is that both witches participate voluntarily,"

Piper informed her. "And I'm not sure Lily is ready to do that."

Juliana sighed. She perched on the edge of a leather-bound trunk where Piper kept extra blankets. "You mean because Lily says she doesn't want to be a shapeshifter," she said.

Piper nodded. "If Lily truly doesn't want Drew's power to transfer to her, the spell won't work."

"It's such a strong power," Juliana said. "I thought firestarting was a big deal. When I received my power, the only other O'Farrell witches alive were my aunt and my grandfather. My aunt could read minds—just a little, you know? Like she could always tell if a guy really liked you or not. Or where you left the keys you lost."

Piper smiled. "Sometimes I wish Phoebe's premonitions worked that way. It might be kinda helpful."

"It was. And she made a living from it," Juliana said. "She had a little booth that she'd set up wherever we went. She told people she was reading their palms, but she was really reading their minds."

"And your grandfather?" Piper asked. She found Juliana's stories fascinating. The O'Farrells had such a different history from her own. It was odd to think there could be such diverse experiences among witch families.

"He had telekinesis," Juliana said. "But it

only worked when he was really emotional. If he was angry or frightened, he could throw an object or two with his mind. Nothing like what Paige does."

"Our oldest sister had that power too," Piper told her. Prue hadn't needed extreme emotions, though—she'd been a strong witch with excellent control over her powers.

"But then, when I could start fires, they were both so proud of me," Juliana said. "I was the strongest witch to be born into our family in years. I got kind of full of myself. I figured if I was strong enough to do that, I'd be strong enough to have a daughter, strong enough to vanquish Gortag and set us all free. But it didn't work," she added sadly.

"Juliana, starting fires with your mind—that's a really strong power," Piper said. "If you weren't a good witch, you could be very dangerous."

"It's nothing compared to what you and your sisters can do," Juliana said. "And it's nothing compared to what Drew just did out there. If that's Lily's power . . ."

"Then maybe you two really can vanquish Gortag," Piper finished for her. "But is that all you want? If Lily doesn't want that kind of power, are you going to make her accept it just so you can get your demon?"

"I just don't understand why she *wouldn't* want to be that powerful," Juliana admitted. "I was thrilled when I realized I had a serious power."

Piper wished Phoebe were here to use her psychology degree. She wasn't sure exactly how to say what she thought without the risk of offending Juliana. "You raised Lily to be afraid of Gortag," she said gently. "All her life, you were hiding, running away. She grew up waiting for the day that she would get her powers, because then the two of you would conquer Gortag. But that's a lot of pressure for Lily. She'd never even seen a demon, and you were just waiting for her to be a powerful witch like you. She was afraid she'd let you down."

Juliana listened carefully, but then she shook her head. "How *can* she let me down?" she asked. "You saw Lily's power—what Drew did out there was incredible. I'm not sure exactly how we're supposed to combine our powers against Gortag, but I know her power is strong enough."

"Her power might be, but maybe *she* isn't," Piper said. "Maybe she's afraid she can't control it. Maybe she's afraid that if she turns into a mouse or a lion that she won't be able to get back. Maybe she's afraid that once you two vanquish Gortag, you won't care about her anymore."

"What?" Juliana cried. "How could she ever think such a thing? She's my only child. She's the most important thing in the world to me!"

"I know," Piper said. "But from something Lily said this morning, I'm not sure she realizes that. She thought you only wanted her so you could use her powers against Gortag."

The color drained from Juliana's face. "She said that?"

Piper nodded. "She was acting out. I doubt she really means it. . . ." She wasn't sure exactly how to comfort Juliana, who was devastated.

"I want to vanquish Gortag so that Lily can live in peace, without fear," she said. "That's the only reason. I just want her to be safe."

"I'm sure that's true, Juliana," Piper told her. "But you focused so much on getting her ready for her powers. She felt that the powers were all that mattered to you."

"Even if she had no powers, I would love her just as much," Juliana said.

"I think you should go tell her that," Piper said. "It might help her overcome her fear of being a powerful shapeshifting witch."

"I don't know about that," Juliana replied. "Even though I thought my power was strong, I've still spent my life being afraid."

"You managed to conquer your fear of Gortag today enough for you to be able to fight him," Piper pointed out. "And you stepped right in front of a charging lion to protect Lily."

"That's different," Juliana said. "It was just Drew, even though she looked like a lion. I knew she'd never hurt me."

"You're pretty close to her, huh?" Piper said.

"They've been friends since they were little,"

Juliana said. "Drew is like another daughter to me."

"I'm sure that helps make up for her crazy parents," Piper replied. "Have you met them?"

Juliana's expression grew troubled. "Only once or twice," she said. "They're not very social. I know Drew doesn't like them much, but I've never seen signs of abuse or neglect. I just get a bad feeling about them."

"Me too," Piper said. "And I've seen them say nasty things to Drew. It's a good thing she has you and Lily to be a positive influence on her."

"I hope they've gotten over their fight," Juliana commented.

Piper thought back to some of the rows that had taken place between her sisters over the years. "It doesn't matter how big the fight is," she said. "The girlbond is stronger."

"Let's hope so," Juliana said. She stood up and straightened her sweater. "I'm going to have a talk with Lily, to see if I can convince her that her powers are her birthright. She shouldn't fear them, she should embrace them."

"As long as she knows you'll love her even if she doesn't," Piper reminded her.

"Absolutely." Juliana frowned. "But if she doesn't want to accept them, the transfer spell won't work, right?"

"Right," Piper confirmed.

"Then what happens to Drew?" Juliana asked, worried. "She's not supposed to have this kind of power. She isn't ready for it."

"I know," Piper said again. "That's something we may have to face."

"And we'll have to help her," Juliana said.

"We will," Piper said. "I promise."

"Any luck?" Paige asked Phoebe, sticking her head into the kitchen. Her sister had been trying to finish her vanquishing spell for almost an hour.

"Not really," Phoebe replied glumly. She sat hunched over her journal, and Paige could see several lines crossed out on the page. "I just don't know enough about Gortag. Like, how does he generate his new bodies?"

Paige pictured Gortag in her mind. She'd seen him leave a body, and she'd seen several new bodies appear. But each time, they showed up fully formed. She had no idea where they came from. "I'm not really sure," she admitted, glancing over her shoulder to check on Lily and Drew in the living room. Somehow she didn't think they'd run away again—both girls were shell-shocked by Drew's lion attack on Lily. Neither one of them had said a word since then.

Paige decided to risk it. She slipped into a kitchen chair near Phoebe, making sure she could see the girls in the living room from where she sat. "Okay, so what do we know so far?" she asked.

"We're working on the theory that he leaves his body, skips off into another dimension, makes a new body, and comes back," Phoebe said.

"Maybe we can prevent him from getting back to his dimension," Paige said. "Do you think he shimmers there?"

Phoebe shook her head. "If he was shimmering, we'd see it. He gets there in some other way."

"Can he be in two dimensions at once?" Paige said, thinking out loud. "Maybe the true Gortag is always in his lair in some other dimension, and the bodies we see are like puppets that he controls with his mind."

"Demon body remote control?" Phoebe asked skeptically.

Paige stuck out her tongue at her sister. "It's possible," she said.

"I know," Phoebe replied. "That's the problem. Anything's possible. We have nothing to go on except what we've seen him do today."

"I wonder why the Book of Shadows doesn't have any information about him," Paige said. Usually the book seemed to magically produce the answers they were looking for. On those few occasions when it couldn't help them, Paige always suspected that the book was holding back, as if it wanted them to learn a lesson on their own for some reason.

"I'm thinking it's because he's spent all his life hunting the O'Farrells and nobody else," Phoebe said. "That might be why the Elders can't tell us more about him—because they're not allowed to help Juliana since she renounced them. It's too bad the O'Farrells don't have a Book of Shadows. All Juliana knows about him is that he's got mind control and can only be vanquished by a mother-daughter team."

Paige thought back to her reading on Wiccan history. When she first learned she was a witch, she'd done a fair amount of research on her new calling. As far as she could remember, a lot of witches were superstitious about writing things down, just like the O'Farrells. But often that meant there was a strong oral history—people handing valuable information down from generation to generation, usually in the form of stories. "I wonder if Juliana and Lily know more about Gortag than they think," she said, pushing back her chair.

"Where are you going?" Phoebe yelped. "I need help!"

"I'm hoping Lily can give you some," Paige said. "Come on."

Phoebe followed her into the living room. One look at the teenagers showed Paige that the girls still hadn't made up. They sat on opposite ends of the couch, not looking at each other. Drew was twisting a strand of brown hair around her finger, and Lily was chipping pink sparkly nail polish off her thumb.

"Okay, you guys, time for a truce," Paige announced. "We need your help."

Both girls looked up, interested. "I thought we were just waiting for a transfer-of-powers spell," Lily said.

"We are," Paige replied. "Your mom and Piper are still upstairs preparing. But in the meantime, you need to help us figure out how to fight Gortag."

"I'm supposed to combine my power with Mom's," Lily said nervously. "That's all I know."

"Good luck," Drew murmured.

Paige ignored her.

"Do you know anything else about Gortag?" Paige asked. "Not about how to vanquish him, but just family stories or bits of trivia."

"Anything at all," Phoebe put in. "We're trying to gather as much info about him as possible."

Lily looked miserable. "I always hated the Gortag stories," she admitted. "I was hoping he never found us, even after I got my powers."

"I remember a story," Drew said unexpectedly. "Lily's mom can start fires with her mind, and there was one story about an O'Farrell who escaped from Gortag by setting him on fire. I guess it didn't kill him, but it slowed him down."

Phoebe narrowed her eyes, thinking. "But Juliana has set Gortag on fire several times today," Paige reminded her. "It doesn't seem to bother him at all."

"This was a really big fire," Lily put in, warming up to the story. "I remember now. It was a witches' bonfire."

"We used to pile up all the red and orange towels we could find and dance around them, pretending it was a bonfire," Drew said, grinning at Lily.

"Yeah, because we loved this story," Lily agreed. "There was a meeting of all the traveling witch families in Ireland at the end of the 1800s."

"And there was a bonfire that they danced around," Drew went on. "They were celebrating the summer solstice."

"Then Gortag attacked, and one of the witches used her power to throw him into the fire," Lily added. "They did a spell to hold him in there, and he stayed. He kept trying to get out, but he couldn't."

"He would stick his arm out and then it would disappear," Drew said. "And then someone would see his tail, but that would disappear too."

"By the time he crawled out of the fire, all the witches had run away," Lily concluded.

Paige had to smile—the girls were finishing each other's sentences the way best friends usually did. She had a feeling that things would be back to normal between them after this.

"Maybe Gortag can take fire for a little while, but if it lasts for too long, he gets weak," Phoebe said.

Paige thought back to their fight with Gortag outside the car. "When Juliana set his whole body on fire this afternoon, he left the body, remember? His spirit kind of jumped out of the body and went away."

"So?" Phoebe asked.

"So . . . he didn't come back for a while," Paige replied. "But when he attacked outside the library, there was a new body every time the old one got killed."

"You mean when there's fire, it takes him longer to make a new body?" Phoebe asked.

"It's like a blown circuit," Paige said, beginning to get excited. For the first time, she thought she might have an idea of how to defeat this demon. "If he goes off and makes a new body every time he loses the old one, he has to be using some kind of power to generate the new body."

"Right," Phoebe said. "It takes energy to create the body."

"But if you have a fuse, and too much electricity goes into the fuse, it blows," Paige said. "It takes a little while for the fuse to reset itself."

"You lost me," Phoebe told her.

Paige wasn't entirely sure she knew what she was talking about either. But she charged ahead, thinking it out as she spoke. "There are different kinds of energy—batteries, electricity, water, solar, wind, fire."

"The elements," Phoebe said.

"Exactly. So let's say he uses heat energy to make his new bodies," Paige went on. "He uses a set amount of heat. But if he's surrounded by fire, it overloads his circuits. He has to shut down for a little while."

"You're saying that our devil can't stand fire," Phoebe said.

"Well, not for very long, anyway," Paige said. "I think the fire keeps him from being able to make a new body. At least he can't do it as efficiently."

"So we need a sustained fire," Phoebe said. "Lots of fuel to burn."

"But that didn't work," Drew piped up. "He was weak, but he still lived through it."

She had a point. Still, Paige didn't think they had anything else to go on. "Listen, we've got a spell to bind his spirit into one body, right?"

Phoebe nodded.

"So if we do that and then we stick the body in the fire, he'll be killed, won't he? I mean, as long as he can't switch bodies?"

"I don't know," Phoebe said slowly.

"It has to be something about fire—why else would that story have been passed down through the O'Farrell family?"

"I just liked the part about a bunch of witches dancing around a fire," Lily said.

"Yeah, it sounded like fun," Drew agreed. "At least until the demon showed up."

"There's always a party pooper," Paige told her. "But usually stories don't get handed down unless there's something to be learned from them."

"And we're forgetting the simplest thing," Phoebe put in. "A mother and daughter are supposed to vanquish Gortag. Well, Gortag got weak in the fire once . . . and Juliana is a firestarter. Doesn't seem like a coincidence."

"But he's supposed to be vanquished by *both* their powers," Paige said. "How could changing into animals help vanquish him?"

They all stared at one another, helpless.

"Maybe when the powers go back to Lily, they'll be different," Drew suggested. "Like instead of shapeshifting, she'll be able to shoot laser beams from her eyes or something."

Lily squirmed nervously in her seat. "That doesn't sound much better," she muttered.

Phoebe turned back toward the kitchen. "I guess our plan is to do the binding spell, then toast him in a fire for as long as possible," she said.

Paige sighed. "The sooner we do the power-transfer spell, the better," she said. "Then maybe we can make a better plan to vanquish Gortag."

"We can do the transfer spell right away," Juliana said, coming down the stairs in time to hear Paige's words. "But I'd like to talk to Lily for a minute first."

Lily and Drew were huddled together on the couch, whispering to each other. But when Lily heard her name, she looked up.

"How about we go into the back garden for a sec?" Juliana said. "Drew, will you excuse us?"

Paige couldn't tell who looked more stricken—Lily at having to have an Important Talk with her mom, or Drew, left behind alone.

Chapter
10

Drew couldn't believe the Halliwells' attic. It was the coolest place she'd ever seen. Ever. Not just because the Book of Shadows was here—at least, she could read the spells as she flipped through. Not just because of the different herbs and flowers hung from the rafters to dry, each with an identifying label written in Piper's neat hand. Not even because of the crystals and candles and other magical props scattered about.

It was cool because she could *feel* magic everywhere. It pulsed from the walls and the wooden floor. The Book of Shadows radiated magic. Even the Halliwells' old furniture felt alive with power. Drew took a deep breath, as if she could actually smell magic in the air.

"I know, it's pretty musty," Piper said apologetically. "No matter how long I leave the windows open, it never airs out. I guess smelling musty is an attic requirement."

Drew shook her head. "I love it," she said. "It smells like witches."

"I didn't know we had a *smell*." Piper peeked out the stained glass window. Drew thought she seemed nervous.

"Is this a hard spell to do?" she asked.

Piper put a hand on her arm, concerned. "No. It will be fine. Are you scared about it?"

Drew was taken aback. She wasn't used to people being worried about her feelings. Well, except the O'Farrells. "Um . . . no," she said. "I'm not scared. I can't wait."

Piper relaxed. "Yeah, I guess you're tired of this witchy stuff," she said. "It'll be nice to get back to normal."

Actually, the thought of *normal* was sort of depressing, Drew realized. "Not really," she said. "I just think the spell itself will be fun. I like to feel magic happening. Orbing with you guys was fun, and turning into animals was fun. I mean, until I attacked Lily. Then it was scary. But I liked the tingly magic feeling."

"I like that too," Piper told her. "You never really get used to it. It's always cool."

"It won't be the same just watching Lily do stuff," Drew said sadly. "I wish we could both have powers."

Piper looked at her thoughtfully. "It sounds

as if you've always been really interested in Lily's Wiccan heritage," she said.

"Yeah," Drew replied. "At least she has a heritage. I don't even know where my parents are from. They never talk. I wish I had a family like Lily's. I don't know what her problem is with being a witch."

"Maybe because Lily has no choice about it," Piper said, "she might feel that it's a burden."

Drew rolled her eyes. "Some burden! Having her powers is the only thing I've ever really enjoyed. And now I have to give them back." She couldn't help feeling a little jealous of Lily, who would get to shapeshift for the rest of her life.

"Drew, this spell won't work unless you and Lily both want to transfer the powers from you to her," Piper said seriously. "It doesn't really sound as if you want that."

Drew felt a blush creeping up her cheeks. She knew Piper thought she was some kind of juvenile delinquent, but she knew she wasn't and wanted to prove it—for some reason Drew still wanted to impress Piper and her family. And now she'd managed to give Piper the impression that she would willingly keep her friend's powers.

"Lily is my best friend forever," she said. "I would never steal her powers. They're hers, so I want her to have them back." She meant every word. But she felt a little tug at her heart when she thought of how it would feel to have the power leave her body. "I just wish I had my own powers too," she added quietly.

Phoebe bounced her leg up and down as she perched on the bottom step of the staircase. She was getting impatient. Once they did the spell to give Lily back her powers, they would still have to face Gortag. Paige was peering out the front door right now, looking for him. Phoebe could feel the nervousness from both of her sisters. And she shared it. Somehow she knew that the protection spell they'd done was wearing off. The house didn't feel as safe as it had even an hour ago.

That was the problem with spells; you never knew how long they were going to last. Sometimes one spell did the trick for good, and other times the agents of evil managed to find a way around even the strongest incantation. And Gortag was a tricky demon; Phoebe felt sure he'd manage to worm his way through their house protection spell sooner or later. After all, he was on the hunt for Juliana and Lily. *And it's our fault he knows they exist,* she thought glumly.

Paige was pacing in the living room. "Can't they talk *after* the power-transfer spell?" she asked anxiously.

Phoebe shrugged. They'd been waiting for Lily and Juliana to come back in from the garden for at least ten minutes. Whatever they were discussing, it must be important. Piper had forbidden anyone to interrupt the mother and daughter.

"Are you sure they're still out there?" she asked Paige. Interrupting was one thing, but keeping the O'Farrells safe was another. Paige stalked through the foyer and into the kitchen to look out the back door. She returned a few seconds later and plopped onto the step next to Phoebe.

"Yeah, they're deep in conversation," Paige reported. "Wonder what it's about."

"I think Juliana's trying to talk Lily into *wanting* to be a witch. If she doesn't truly want her powers, the transfer spell won't work."

Paige's brown eyes were troubled. "I'm not sure anyone will be able to talk Lily into that," she said. "I got the feeling that she's not thrilled about her witchy heritage."

"Neither were you," Phoebe pointed out. In fact, none of her sisters had been thrilled to learn they were witches. She herself was the only one who'd thought it was pretty cool right away. Piper and Prue hadn't even believed in witches to begin with, and when Paige had come into the fold, she'd thought the Halliwells were just crazy.

"Yeah, but Lily seemed almost afraid of taking on the shapeshifting power," Paige said. "You saw her after Drew's lion attack."

"I know," Phoebe said. "She seemed just as

freaked out by the idea of turning into a lion as she was by being attacked by one."

"What will happen if the transfer doesn't work?" Paige asked. "Is it safe for Drew to be stuck with powers she's not supposed to have?"

Phoebe thought about it. Drew actually seemed to be handling her sudden power pretty well. "I think it will be okay for a little while," she said. "But we can't leave her that way for good. Lily's just going to have to accept her destiny."

White light filled the air, and Leo orbed in. He didn't look happy.

"What is it?" Phoebe asked.

"I tried to get through a loophole with the Elders," Leo said. "I thought they could help Lily even though Juliana had turned her back on them."

"And?" Paige asked.

"And all they'll say is that this is a test of character for the O'Farrell family. They won't help Juliana's daughter until she asks them for help as a full-fledged witch herself."

"Who, Lily?" Phoebe said. "Why don't we tell her to ask them for help, then? Juliana has a grudge against them, but she didn't teach it to Lily."

"It won't work," Leo sighed. "Not until she's a witch."

"You mean not until *after* the power-transfer spell," Paige said.

Leo nodded. "They did give me one other piece of information about Gortag, though."

Phoebe studied his face. "And I'm guessing it wasn't good news," she said.

"You know how they told me the same prophecy that Juliana heard?" he replied. "Well, this time I asked them exactly how the mother-daughter thing was supposed to work, so we'd know how to vanquish him right away when the transfer spell is done."

"Good idea," said Phoebe. "So what's the problem?"

"They said it's a very individual thing. The mother and daughter have to use their specific powers in combination, and even the Elders can't see the combination."

"You mean they can't just say a vanquishing spell together?" Paige asked.

Leo shook his head. "They're just going to have to figure it out on the fly."

"At least we'll all be there to help them," Phoebe said.

The kitchen door opened, sending its familiar squeak sounding through the foyer. Instantly Phoebe and Paige leaped to their feet. Phoebe tried to control her impatience as Juliana and Lily made their way to the stairs. If Lily was already feeling pressured by her mom, the last thing she needed was pressure from the Charmed Ones.

"All set?" Phoebe asked with a smile.

"I think so," Juliana answered, her own smile a bit uncertain.

"Where's Drew?" Lily asked.

"Upstairs with Piper," Paige replied. "They're just waiting for you, and we can begin the spell."

Lily took a deep breath. "Okay," she said. Phoebe exchanged a relieved smile with Paige. She stepped back to allow Lily to lead the way upstairs.

The O'Farrells were only five steps up when the front door burst open as if someone had rigged it with dynamite.

Phoebe whirled around to see what had happened. In the open doorway stood Gortag.

She stared at him wordlessly for a moment. *Guess I was right about that protection spell wearing off,* she thought. Then everything happened at once. Gortag charged forward, his yellow eyes locked on Lily. Paige rushed up the steps, grabbed the teenager, and orbed her away. And Phoebe spun around and delivered a round-house kick right to Gortag's chest.

"Run!" she told Juliana and Leo as Gortag staggered backward. "Start the transfer spell!"

Leo held out his hand to Juliana. This time she reacted instantly, placing her hand in his. They orbed away. And Phoebe turned to face the demon, alone.

Chapter

11

Lily tried to catch her breath as she and Paige orbed into the Halliwells' attic. She only caught one glimpse of Gortag before Paige grabbed her, but it was enough to undo everything she and her mom had talked about in the garden.

Juliana had tried to convince her that she didn't care whether or not Lily accepted her powers. She'd said that Lily's happiness was more important to her than anything, even vanquishing Gortag. And Lily knew that was true. She had even been leaning toward refusing her powers and asking the Charmed Ones to help them figure out how to relieve Drew of the powers without transferring them to Lily.

But now that Gortag was here again, Lily suddenly understood. He was *never* going to stop chasing them. Even if she and her mom went back into hiding, he would come after them. And they wouldn't always have the Halliwells to help get rid of him. He had to be vanquished. Which meant that she had to accept her destiny—she had to become a witch. And it didn't matter whether she wanted to or not. It was her duty. For the first time, Lily felt she really understood why all the O'Farrells before her had asked for their powers. It was so they'd be strong enough to defend themselves.

Piper and Drew were gathered around the Book of Shadows. Piper looked up, alarmed, when she caught sight of them.

"What's going on?" she cried.

"Gortag's here," Paige said. "We have to do the transfer spell *now*." She shepherded Lily into one of the two whitish circles on the floor. Drew ran into the other one.

Lily's heart was pounding with fear. Where was her mother? Still downstairs fighting Gortag? And what did these circles mean? "What is this?" she asked Drew. "Are they protection circles?"

"Yeah," Drew said. "Once the spell starts we can't step out of them or else—"

"Or else we break the chain of magic," she finished. She felt calmer just talking to Drew. All her life, she'd discussed her Wiccan heritage with her best friend. But she'd never told Drew about the actual magic spells that Juliana showed her. After all, it was forbidden by the O'Farrells' ancient clan to divulge the secrets of family magic to an outsider. But today Drew had seen more magic than any non-Wiccan ever should. There was so much going on that Lily felt overwhelmed, even with all her training. But Drew seemed completely comfortable. She even seemed sort of excited by all the magic.

"Where's your mom?" Drew asked, worried.

"Fighting Gortag," Lily replied.

"We better switch the powers to you fast," Drew cried. "You have to use them to help her vanquish that jerk."

Lily swallowed hard. She could barely get her mind around the fact that she would be a shapeshifter in a few minutes. How was she supposed to figure out how to use her new powers fast enough to vanquish Gortag? Were they really expecting her to vanquish a dangerous demon in her first five minutes as a witch? Fear threatened to overwhelm her.

Leo orbed into the attic with Juliana, her eyes wide with alarm. She looked at Drew and Lily in their circles, then at Piper standing with the Book of Shadows. "Start the spell!" she cried.

"I'm going as fast as I can," Piper said, carefully placing a large, shallow bowl full of water on the clean-swept floor. She made sure no drops of water had fallen onto the wood.

"Okay, let's go," she said, joining Paige at the podium that held the Book of Shadows. Together, Piper and Paige read from the book:

Sun and moon, earth and water,
Smile now upon your daughters.
Each one wants what the other holds.
Reverse their power, exchange their molds.

The white circles on the floor began to glow with a shimmering light. Lily felt as if someone had suddenly turned a heat lamp on her. She turned to look at Drew. Her best friend was grinning, eyes shining. "Can you feel that tingling?" Drew called.

Lily nodded. There was a tingling in her hands and feet. It felt sort of like the pins and needles you got when your leg fell asleep. Not really painful, but not really pleasant either.

"Juliana, your part," Piper called.

Lily's mom was stationed in front of the door to the attic. She'd been staring down the stairs, on guard for any sign of Gortag. Now she turned and ran over to the podium holding the Book of Shadows. She read aloud:

Ancestor witches, hear your daughter's plea.
Send one to judge whose these powers
should be.

Lily noticed that the water in the bowl had begun to spill over the edges, forming a strange puddle on the clean-swept wooden floor in between her circle and Drew's. As she watched, the puddle grew larger, until it looked like a miniature pool right in the middle of the attic. Suddenly all the water from the pool rose five feet into the air. Not like a fountain, though. To Lily it looked more like an ice sculpture, a statue made of water. Then the water solidified, and she found herself staring at a woman. An old, old woman with long white hair and big green eyes set in a wrinkled face.

"Who calls me?" she asked in a creaky voice.

"I do," Juliana replied. "My daughter's power has been given to another. I want it returned to its rightful owner."

The old woman began to laugh, a strange squeaky sound like two rocks grating against each other. A shiver ran up Lily's spine. Who was this woman? Was she one of their ancestors, an O'Farrell? *She could be my great-grandmother*, Lily thought. *Or my great-great-great-grandmother . . .* It was hard to imagine that there was a whole line of O'Farrell witches out there somewhere, wherever witches went when they died. Lily had spent her whole life knowing that she and her mom were alone, with no family left at all. But now she stood looking at family. Suddenly she felt at peace.

The old woman turned to her and stared searchingly into her eyes. "Only a witch herself can ask for a transfer of powers," she said, talking to Juliana while looking at Lily. "You cannot ask it for her."

Lily tried to sound as confident and strong as

her mother had when she read the spell. "I ask it, ancestor witch," she said. "My power has been given to another. I want it back."

The old woman's lips twitched as she continued to stare at Lily. Then suddenly she spun to Drew. "You are the one with power," she said. "You are the one who must ask."

Drew took a deep breath. Lily thought she looked sad. "I . . . ," she began, but her voice broke. "I don't want to give up these powers," she announced.

"Two Gortags down, a million more to go," Phoebe muttered. The first Gortag body had been killed by a well-aimed blow to the neck. The second one had appeared almost immediately, and Phoebe had taken it out by levitating over its head and tackling it from above. She waited for the next one to appear. Nothing happened.

Then she heard footsteps on the stairs above her. *It's Gortag*, she realized. He must've materialized his new body on the way up to the attic. Phoebe raced up the steps as fast as she could run. The spell to bind Gortag into one body was in the pocket of her jeans, but it needed the Power of Three to activate it. She had to get to her sisters. She could only hope they'd managed to transfer Drew's powers to Lily. Otherwise, Lily would be defenseless.

As she rounded the bend in the staircase, she caught sight of Gortag's red tail running up ahead of her. Putting on a burst of speed, she leaped a few steps up and grabbed his tail, pulling as hard as she could. He tumbled backward down the stairs, and Phoebe jumped over his arm as he tried to grab her leg on the way down.

"You cannot defeat Gortag!" he yelled as he fell.

"We'll see about that," she retorted, running up the second staircase to the attic. She rushed through the door and stopped, surprised. Some old lady was standing in between Drew and Lily in their glowing protective circles.

"Who's that?" she whispered to Leo, who stood near the door.

"One of the O'Farrell ancestors," he whispered back. "She's the mediator in charge of transferring their powers."

"Well, is she almost done?" Phoebe asked, glancing over her shoulder. "Because Gortag's on his way up."

"No." Leo looked a little embarrassed. "There's a holdup."

"What? Why?"

"Listen," Leo said, nodding toward the girls. Phoebe stepped closer.

"Are you crazy?" Lily was saying. "You have to give them back to me!"

"Do you really want to be a shapeshifter?" Drew asked. "I mean *really*?"

Lily's chin quivered. She shot a worried look

at her mother. "I have to," she said. "I have to help defeat Gortag."

Juliana gasped and started forward, but Paige grabbed her arm. "You can't break the protective circle," Paige warned her.

"Lily, you don't have to take the powers," Juliana cried urgently. "If you don't want them, you don't have to have them. I love you either way. You have to believe me!"

Lily looked at her doubtfully. "What about Gortag?"

"Gortag will kill you!" a voice trumpeted from behind Phoebe. Before she could even turn, Piper exploded him.

"He'll be back," Phoebe called.

But Juliana ignored her. In fact, she ignored everything in the room except her daughter. "Lily, I love *you*, not your powers. We'll find some other way to defeat Gortag. Or we'll go back into hiding from him. You have to make up your mind for yourself. Do you want your powers?"

Lily hesitated. Phoebe held her breath. It wouldn't be easy for the girl to make such a momentous decision on the spot.

Gortag appeared near the window in back of Paige and Piper. "Behind you!" Phoebe yelled to her sisters. Once again, Piper turned to explode him, but Gortag was too fast. He grabbed Juliana and spun her around to face him. Before Phoebe could shout a warning, she saw Juliana lock eyes with the demon.

Uh-oh, now he's going to put the demonic whammy on Juliana, she thought. They'd have not only a demon to fight, but a firestarting witch, as well.

"Mom!" Lily cried, horrified.

"Help me kill the Charmed Ones," Gortag said conversationally.

Juliana nodded. "Sure, I'll help." She turned to Paige and grabbed her wrist. Paige orbed away. Frowning, Juliana turned to Piper. Piper threw up her hands and froze Juliana and Gortag, who stood behind her.

"What's going on?" Lily cried, terrified. "Why is my mother fighting you?"

"It's Gortag's psychic powers," Phoebe explained, running to her older sister. Paige orbed back in just as she got there.

"Hey," Paige said. "How'd you freeze Juliana? She's a good witch."

Piper shrugged. "She's not good at the moment. She's under Gortag's control," she replied. "How do we reverse his hold on her?"

"When he had Phoebe like that, I just did a release spell," Paige replied. "But I had to look into her eyes."

Someone cleared her throat. They all turned to see the O'Farrell ancestor frowning at them like a disapproving schoolteacher.

"Uh, we're in the middle of something here," Phoebe called. "Can you wait just a sec?"

"No, let's finish it now," said Lily, her voice

stronger than Phoebe had ever heard it. "That demon is brainwashing my mother," she said. "I want to vanquish him."

Gortag stirred, and Juliana set the drapes on fire. "Piper!" Phoebe yelped.

"Sorry," her sister replied, refreezing them. Leo pulled down the flaming curtain and stamped out the flames.

Lily stared at Drew. "You have to give me my powers back," she said.

"I will," Drew said slowly. "As long as you're sure you want them."

"I want them."

Drew looked into the old woman's eyes. "I have another's power. I want you to give it back."

Phoebe waited for a magic wind to blow. In fact, she waited for anything to happen. But the old woman just kept studying Drew. "No," she said.

Chapter

12

"Excuse me?" Paige said. She couldn't believe she'd heard right.

"I will not transfer these powers," the old woman said calmly.

Paige glanced at her sisters. Piper was watching Gortag and Juliana, freezing them every time her previous freeze wore off. And Phoebe was on high alert, ready to judo chop anyone who moved. But both of them looked about a half second away from turning their powers on this old O'Farrell witch.

"But I *want* them now," Lily cried. "I really do!" She shot Drew an accusing look.

"And I want you to have them," Drew said hastily. "You need them to save your mom. I want you to save her. I do."

Poor kid doesn't think anyone will believe her, Paige thought, surprised to find that she did believe Drew. After all, she'd avoided hurting Juliana even as an angry lion. If she had to give up playing witch to help Juliana now, she would.

"We're asking you to transfer them," Lily tried again.

"No," the old lady replied. Her solid form began to liquefy, just a bit. Paige stopped her when she reached Jell-O consistency.

"Hold it right there," she said. "You're gonna have to explain all this before you leave. Why won't you do what they ask?"

"Only one born to be a witch can wield such an enormous power," said the old woman. Water ran in droplets from her hair and skin. "This power would destroy the nonwitch."

Paige's eyes flew to Drew. "But that's exactly why we want you to transfer the power," she argued. "If it's going to destroy Drew, you have to give the powers back to Lily."

The old woman smiled, the edges of her lips melting away as she spoke. "Do you think I don't recognize my own kind?" she asked. Her voice had begun to gurgle as if she were underwater. She turned her watery gaze on Drew. "That one is the witch."

"What?" cried Paige.

But the old woman was dissolving too fast to answer. Her face had become transparent, and now it liquefied entirely, collapsing straight down to the floor. The water moved back toward the bowl, flowing over the rim like a wave. She was gone.

Paige stared at the bowl of water as if she could just will the O'Farrell ancestor to come back and explain herself.

Suddenly Phoebe screamed. Paige whirled around to find her sister's sleeve on fire. "Sleeve!" Paige cried, orbing the flaming sleeve right off Phoebe's shirt and straight into the bowl of water.

Phoebe didn't even have time to thank her because Gortag launched himself at her, fists swinging. Phoebe blocked his blows and started fighting back, making sure not to look in his eyes.

"Piper!" Paige cried. "What's going on?"

"I was listening to the old lady and I didn't notice the freeze wear off," Piper said. "Sorry." Juliana set the podium holding the Book of Shadows on fire.

"Do something!" Juliana cried. "I can't stop myself!"

Paige grabbed the bowl of water and threw it on the fire, while Piper jumped in front of Juliana. "Goddess, hear my call. Release!" she commanded.

Juliana slumped to the ground like a marionette whose strings had been cut. "Mom!" Lily cried, running over to hug her. Juliana weakly returned her embrace.

Paige took stock of the situation. Gortag was

still fighting with Phoebe, and Leo had joined in. Juliana and Lily were safe for the moment, and Drew still stood in her protective circle, face blank with shock.

"What should I do?" Piper asked. "Should I explode him?"

"We have a spell to bind him in one body," Paige murmured, not wanting Gortag to hear.

"So we do that and then I explode him?" Piper asked.

"Yeah. Or else we stick him in a fire for a long time," Paige said. "We're not exactly sure how he works yet."

"You will protect me," Gortag boomed.

Uh-oh. It sounded like Gortag had found another mental victim. She looked over to see him staring into Leo's eyes, as if hypnotizing him.

"Can he do that to a Whitelighter?" she asked.

Leo turned and punched Phoebe in the stomach. "Ow!" she yelled, outraged.

"Yup," Piper answered Paige. "Leo!" He glanced up when he heard his name. "Goddess, hear our call. Release!" Paige and Piper said together.

Leo stumbled backward, but then glanced up with a smile. "Thanks," he said. "That was weird."

"Drew!" yelled Lily. "Watch out!"

Gortag had given up on Phoebe and was now running straight at Drew in her magic circle.

"The circle won't protect her now that the spell has ended," Paige said. Piper raised her hands and exploded Gortag as he ran. A new Gortag appeared almost instantaneously, still rushing at Drew.

Paige launched herself across the room, grabbed Drew by the arm, and orbed them to the living room. The movement seemed to shake Drew out of her shock.

"What's going on?" she cried.

"I'm not sure," Paige admitted. "But I think we'd better keep you away from Gortag."

"But Lily and her mom are up there," Drew protested. "I have to help them!" Before Paige could stop her, the girl took off running for the stairs.

"Teenagers," Paige muttered, orbing back up to the attic. Gortag was just ducking under a blow from Leo, who stood in front of Juliana and Lily, ready to orb them to safety.

"Thank god you're back," Phoebe greeted her. "Let's do the binding spell." She pulled a slip of crumpled paper out of her pocket and held it in front of Piper and Paige. They all read together:

Demon of many bodies,
Spirit of one,
In this form we command you, Stay!

Gortag let out a howl as their magic hit him. "Quick, explode him!" Paige cried. Piper raised her hands and blew him up just as Drew charged into the room.

Paige bent over, trying to catch her breath. "I'm glad that's over with," she said.

"Is he vanquished?" Drew asked.

Paige nodded.

"I can't believe it," Juliana said in a trembling voice. She was still huddled on the floor, her arms around Lily. "I can't believe he's really gone. My family is avenged."

For a moment everyone was silent. Paige knew they were all thinking the same thing. Why hadn't the O'Farrell ancestor switched Drew's powers to Lily? But who would have the courage to speak up first?

"Why didn't the transfer spell work?" Lily asked in a small voice.

"That old lady said I was a witch," Drew said. "But Lily's the witch."

"Maybe she wasn't a true ancestor," Juliana said. "The spell could've gone wrong."

"Listen, lady, I thought you trusted us by now," Phoebe said. "We know what we're doing. The spell didn't go wrong."

"Then why didn't it work?" Juliana asked.

"Does it really matter?" asked Gortag. Paige jumped as she noticed the devil-like demon for the first time. He stood in the doorway of the attic, leaning casually against the frame.

Lily screamed, but Paige was too shocked to do anything but stare at him.

"I thought he was vanquished," Phoebe cried.

"From your little binding spell?" Gortag asked. "Stupid witch! Many have tried such spells before. Gortag cannot be controlled by crude witch magic. Gortag is far too complex for your small minds to comprehend!"

"Yeah, well, Paige is gonna kick Gortag's butt if he doesn't stop referring to himself in the third person," Paige muttered.

"Why didn't *that* work either?" Phoebe asked, turning to Piper. "Nothing works on this jerk."

"Um, Phoebes, I think we have bigger problems right now," Paige interrupted, gesturing to Gortag. He was running at Juliana. Piper exploded him.

But Paige knew there would be another. And another. They hadn't vanquished Gortag—and worse, they obviously didn't have a clue as to how they could.

Chapter

13

The next Gortag appeared. This time he rushed toward Drew. She watched him come, frozen with fear.

"Drew!" Lily screamed. Before Drew could react, Lily jumped in front of Gortag and kicked him in the shin. He raised one scrawny red arm and swatted her to the side.

Drew felt fear coursing through her body—fear, and magic. The transformation began even before Piper exploded this Gortag too. As the demon disappeared Drew felt her skin change, growing iridescent scales all along her arms and legs, spreading to her body and then her face. She grew in height until her head scraped the ceiling. Her teeth lengthened into fangs, and she hiccuped a small burst of fire.

"She's a . . . dragon," Lily said, stepping away from Drew.

Drew wasn't surprised. She hadn't known what she was turning into, but now that the transformation was complete, she *knew* she was a dragon. In fact, she knew everything about being a dragon—how to fly, how to breathe fire, and just where the vulnerable spot was in her armor of scales. But she also knew everything that Drew-the-girl knew. It was like being two different species at once.

I have to turn back, she thought. *I'm scaring Lily.* But how? Drew concentrated on remembering how she'd turned into the dragon in the first place. Gortag was trying to attack her. She'd been afraid, and a small part of her brain had wished she was strong enough to fight him. *That's it!* she realized. Her magic had taken that small wish and interpreted it—she'd turned into a fierce creature who could fight Gortag. So maybe if she wished to be a girl again, it would work.

Drew concentrated, picturing her body the way it normally felt—soft skin, no fire in her lungs, only five feet tall . . . magic coursed through her veins, and she shrunk back into her usual self.

She grinned. "Gortag's not the only one with lots of bodies," she said. "I think I know how to control it now!"

Piper smiled back. "That's great, Drew."

"Duck!" yelled Phoebe. Piper ducked, and so did Drew. Phoebe delivered a strong kick over their heads, knocking down Gortag, who had just materialized right behind Drew.

"We have to deal with him—now!" Juliana cried, running over. She pulled Drew away from Gortag as he climbed back to his feet. "He'll just keep popping back up until we're too exhausted to fight him anymore."

"But I don't know how to give my power back to Lily," Drew protested.

"Maybe it's okay," Piper put in. "The prophecy said he'd be destroyed by a combination of a mother and daughter's powers. Maybe the power is all that matters—it *is* Lily's power, no matter who wields it."

"You mean I can use Lily's power and it will still count?" Drew asked doubtfully.

Piper glanced at Leo, who shrugged. "I guess that could work," he said.

"But we still don't know how to vanquish him," Juliana said hopelessly. Phoebe had just finished beating up another Gortag, and she was panting with exertion. The situation was grim.

Drew thought about the conversation she and Lily had had with Paige and Phoebe earlier. "What about fire?" she asked. "Remember?"

The sisters exchanged a look. "It's worth a try," Paige said. She took cover as Piper exploded Gortag yet again.

"What are you talking about?" Juliana asked.

"Remember the old story about Gortag in the bonfire?" Lily said. "The one where the witches kept him in the fire and it made him weak?"

Juliana nodded.

"Well, we thought maybe the fire short-circuited his ability to make new bodies," Paige told her. "So if we hold him in the fire awhile, he'll at least grow weaker."

"I guess we can try," Juliana said doubtfully. "It may buy us time."

"You have no time!" Gortag bellowed. He materialized in between Drew and Juliana. "Set a fire!" Drew yelled as Gortag grabbed her.

He wasn't any taller than she, and he was really scrawny. Still, Drew was shocked at how strong he was—every inch of his skinny red body was muscle. But he wasn't fighting Drew. He was just trying to make her look into his eyes.

He wants to use his mind control on me, she realized. *He probably wants to make me fight with Lily's mom or something.*

She closed her eyes tight and concentrated on getting away from him. Her body began to shrink, soft feathers sprouting all over. She felt her feet grow long, her toes curl into talons. *A bird!* she thought. Immediately she pumped her wings, yanking herself from Gortag's grasp. She flew to the top of a bookshelf and perched there.

Below her, Piper had set out yet another large bowl, this one made of stone. "Start a fire," Piper told Juliana.

"My power is weak," Juliana said breathlessly. "Gortag made me use it too often before."

"You have to try," Paige told her.

"But I'll have to keep the fire going for a long time," Juliana replied. "I don't know if I can. There's no fuel here, so it will be all magic."

"You can do it," Lily said, slipping her hand into her mother's. "You're the strongest witch in the world."

Juliana smiled gratefully at her.

"And we'll help you," Paige said. "Together the three of us are stronger than any one of us separately. We'll stand with you, Juliana. You can use the Power of Three."

"Look out," Phoebe said grimly. Everyone scattered as Gortag rushed them. Phoebe tripped him, dumping him neatly into the stone bowl. "Now!" Phoebe yelled. She grabbed Juliana's hand, and her sisters rushed to join hands with them as well.

Juliana set Gortag on fire—a huge rush of flame, bigger than anything Drew had ever seen her do before. Gortag let out a yell. But then his body went limp, all the life gone from it.

"Gortag has left the body," Paige cracked.

"So much for that plan," Phoebe said, her voice breaking. "This guy is really starting to tick me off. There has to be some way to get rid of him."

Suddenly Lily turned and looked Drew in the eye. Even with her bird brain, Drew knew what her best friend was thinking. Lily had an idea. Lifting her delicate wings, Drew flew down from the bookshelf to rest on Lily's shoulder.

"Drew turned into a dragon," Lily said.

Paige and Piper looked at her blankly. "We know, honey," Juliana said tiredly.

"No, I mean she turned into something that doesn't really exist," Lily said. "Well, it's not supposed to exist, anyway."

"A mythological creature," Piper put in.

"Yeah," Lily said, excitement creeping into her voice. "So if she can do one mythological creature, she can probably do them all—"

Her words were cut off by the arrival of another Gortag. This one appeared immediately behind Lily. He wrapped his arms around her and yanked her backward toward the window. Startled, Drew flew off her shoulder. "Mom, set him on fire again," Lily called before Gortag slapped his hand over her mouth.

In the air Drew began to change. Lily hadn't finished telling them her plan, but it didn't matter. Drew knew what she was thinking. It was like that with best friends. She felt her wings grow longer, the feathers becoming shimmery. Her beak extended forward, and her body became larger. She was still a bird, but a completely different kind of bird. All her fear of Gortag left her. She was ready to fight him.

Juliana was frantic, tears running down her cheeks as Gortag held on to Lily. No one could use power against him without hurting her as well. Drew dove through the air, aiming at

Gortag's skinny arm. She landed with her sharp talons digging into his flesh, and she pecked at his face as Lily ducked.

With a howl, Gortag released his hold on Lily ever so slightly. Lily rammed her elbow into his side and yanked herself away. "Mom, fire!" she yelled.

Juliana set him on fire again. Piper, Phoebe, and Paige stood in a line with her, lending the Power of Three to Juliana's power. The fire burned with a white-hot fury, even though the ground beneath it was bare. There was nothing to fuel the fire—it was witches' fire.

Drew circled the flaming demon, waiting to see what would happen. Gortag's body went limp again. But this time she noticed a distortion in the air above his head as his body fell. *It's his spirit! I can see it!* she thought excitedly. Without hesitation she flew straight into the flames.

"Drew, no!" Piper screamed. The flames faltered.

"No, Mom, keep him on fire," Lily said urgently. Juliana frowned, trying to squirm away from the Halliwells' grasp.

"Listen to your daughter," Paige said. "We have to keep the fire burning." The flames leaped back up.

Peering through the fire, Drew's sharpened eyesight could easily make out the evil spirit rising from Gortag's body. She stretched out her

talons, gratified to feel them sink into the substance of his invisible self. She held his spirit in
the flames.

As the heat rose around Drew, searing her
flesh, she felt Gortag trying to escape. He
writhed around, but she held tight. He tried to
form a new body, but it collapsed like a lump of
clay. He tried again and got only a pointy tail.
He screamed and screamed, but Drew knew no
one could hear him but her. The heat was
almost unbearable now, and she could smell her
own feathers burning. She couldn't last much
longer. With her dying breath, she held on to the
invisible demon.

And when she died, she knew that he had
died too.

Chapter

14

Piper stared at the pile of ashes in the stone bowl. She felt numb.

Beside her, Juliana sobbed uncontrollably. Paige slipped an arm around the distraught woman's shoulders, but all Piper could think to do was just stare at the ashes.

"Is he gone?" Lily asked, sounding surprisingly calm. "Is Gortag vanquished?"

"I think so," Phoebe replied. "I saw him trying to make new bodies. He couldn't. I think when Drew held him in the flame for so long, he overloaded on energy."

Piper didn't know if that made sense or not. She couldn't get her mind past the fact that Drew was gone. She'd sacrificed herself to vanquish Gortag.

"He *is* vanquished," she realized. "The only way that it could be done was by combining the powers of a mother and daughter. That's exactly what happened. Your powers set him on fire, and when Drew used Lily's power to shapeshift, she was able to hold him in the fire until he died."

"How?" Phoebe asked, asking the question they all had.

"Maybe that bird had a higher tolerance for the heat and smoke?" Paige suggested. "But why would that be?"

"I don't know," Leo said. "But it almost looked like she could see his spirit form, his true self."

"It was magic," Lily said matter-of-factly. Piper studied the girl. She was sitting calmly on the floor next to the pile of ashes. Staring at the ashes. But not crying or shaking or acting upset at all. *She's in shock,* Piper thought. They all were.

Leo came over and hugged her. She pressed her face into his shirt, trying to block out the fact that they'd just watched an innocent thirteen-year-old girl die.

"What are we going to tell Drew's parents?" she asked, pulling back.

"Nothing," Lily said.

Juliana went over and sat next to Lily. "We have to tell them something, honey," she said gently. "Drew's gone. You realize that, don't you?"

"Sure," Lily replied, keeping her eyes on the ashes.

Piper didn't know what to make of it. With all they'd been through together, she would have expected Lily to be inconsolable. Maybe she was in denial.

"Let's get this cleaned up," Paige said, heading for the bowl filled with ashes.

"No!" Lily yelled, leaping to her feet. "Don't touch it!"

Paige stopped in her tracks. "Okay," she said quickly. "We'll leave it. Whatever you want."

Juliana looked at Lily with worried eyes. But Lily had begun to smile. "Look," she whispered.

Piper followed her gaze to the stone bowl. Something was moving underneath the ashes, pushing them around in small gray waves.

"Is it Gortag?" Phoebe asked, alarmed. "Maybe he's making a new body."

"It's Drew," Lily said.

The ashy waves were getting bigger. "What do you mean?" Piper asked, drawn to the strange movement. Now the rolling waves had begun moving outward from the center in concentric circles.

"She's coming back," Lily replied.

"Oh, Lil," Juliana said sadly. "I don't think—"

"What's that?" Paige interrupted. They all leaned closer to the bowl. The ashes had begun bubbling up like a minifountain. As they watched, the fountain shot higher and higher into the air.

Suddenly the ashes burst upward, whirling

and spinning about to form a vertical column of ash. Piper stepped back in surprise. "What's going on?" she asked Leo.

A thundering sound drowned out his answer. The ashes twirled faster and faster, creating a roar like a tornado. Then all at once they burst outward, scattering everywhere as a large shimmering bird launched itself from the ashes and swooped around the attic.

Piper gasped, ducking down as it flew over her head.

"She's a phoenix," Lily said proudly. "She was reborn from the ashes."

Juliana sat back on her heels and watched Drew's flight with a huge smile of relief. "You knew this was going to happen," she said to Lily.

"Yup," the girl replied proudly. "Once she turned into a dragon, I knew she could do this, too. And then she'd be able to hold Gortag in the fire long enough to kill him."

"How did you know about phoenixes?" Paige asked.

"We used to read all kinds of fairy tales and myths when we were little," Drew answered, transforming back into her own body. Lily ran over and threw her arms around her best friend with a happy squeal. Then Juliana did too, embracing both girls.

Piper slipped her arm around Leo's waist as she watched them. "Why didn't the Elders tell you about Drew?" she asked him. "I think she was our true innocent all along."

"I don't know," he said. "Maybe because I only asked them about the O'Farrells."

"What did our ancestor witch mean when she said Drew was the true witch?" Lily asked, her green eyes worried. "She said she didn't recognize me."

Juliana frowned. "Maybe she didn't recognize you because you aren't a witch yet," she suggested.

"But I was trying to get my witch's powers," Lily pointed out.

Silence fell over the room.

Finally Juliana turned to Leo. "The Elders will know the answer, won't they?" she asked.

"I think so," he said. "They only said they couldn't help you. They never said they didn't know how to. Now that you're willing to trust good magic again, maybe they can be more forthcoming."

"Then I'll ask them," Juliana whispered.

Leo stared deeply into her big green eyes. "Are you sure, Juliana? You turned your back on them once."

"I know." Juliana took a long look at Lily, and then at Drew. "I was young and I was angry at them. I thought I could do better on my own. But I was wrong."

Piper shifted uncomfortably. She'd certainly had her share of anger toward the Elders over the years. "Juliana, you did fine on your own," she put in. "You raised Lily and kept her safe from Gortag all these years."

"By hiding," Juliana said. "By denying myself the company and the help of other witches. I kept Lily secret, but I don't know about safe." She smiled at Piper. "It was hard for me at first, letting myself trust you guys. But it was the best thing I've ever done. I didn't have to face Gortag alone."

"You vanquished him alone," Piper pointed out. "Well, without us, I mean."

"The fire thing was Paige's idea," Lily said. "And you guys have kept us safe all day—me and Mom *and* Drew."

"It's time for me to rejoin the community of witches," Juliana said. "Lily and I would both be safer and happier if we had our own White-lighter. What do I have to do?" she asked, turning to Leo.

He smiled. "I'll go ask." He orbed out, leaving behind an awkward silence. Piper was glad that Juliana had decided to trust the Elders again. It was nice to know that her own family had played a role in convincing the woman to trust other witches and Whitelighters. But she had a feeling that Juliana wasn't going to like what the Elders had to say.

Chapter

15

"That's impossible," Juliana declared for the fifth time, pacing angrily around the living room.

"That's what the Elders said," Leo insisted. "Drew is your daughter, not Lily."

"They're wrong," Juliana said curtly.

Drew tried not to show how much the words hurt her. She knew Juliana was right—it was impossible that Drew was her daughter. Drew had her own parents, and Juliana had Lily. The Elders had clearly made a mistake. But it was hard to forget the thrill of hope that had shot through her body when Leo orbed in with the news that she was an O'Farrell too. Imagine having Juliana for a mother! Lily for a sister!

That won't happen, Drew told herself. If she was Juliana's real child, it would mean Lily wasn't. They couldn't both be O'Farrells. There couldn't be some kind of happy family ending.

"It makes sense, though," Piper argued gently. "Drew didn't do a power-stealing spell to get Lily's powers. They just came to her naturally."

"But if I'm not a witch," Lily said, "and I'm the one who did the spell to call my powers to me . . . then the spell shouldn't have worked. Not even to call the powers to someone else."

"That's true," Phoebe put in, frowning.

Should I tell them? Drew wondered. She didn't want to make Lily mad at her. But still, she had to tell the truth.

"I said the spell too," she admitted in a small voice.

Everyone turned to look at Drew. Six pairs of eyes bored into her, and she took a step backward. Piper went to stand next to her—she didn't want the poor girl to think she was in trouble and take off again.

"The spell to invoke your powers?" Leo asked gently.

Drew nodded. "I didn't think it would invoke anything in *me*," she said. "But I was watching Lily do the spell, and I thought it was cool. So I repeated it along with her. I didn't mean any harm. I'm sorry."

Juliana looked really pale. Piper wondered if she was going to faint. "Drew said the spell, and the powers came to Drew," Piper said. "It wasn't a mistake. Drew is the true witch."

Silence filled the room. Piper didn't know

what to think. She didn't even know what to hope for. Lily began to cry softly.

"When Lily was born, did you ever let her out of your sight?" Paige asked Juliana.

Juliana shook her head. "No. I mean, when I was sleeping . . . but she was always in a bassinet right next to my bed."

"And I've been with my parents for as long as I can remember," Drew put in.

"I just don't understand how Drew could be my daughter," Juliana said. She reached out to take Drew's hand. "You know I've always considered you like a sister to Lily, honey," she said gently. "But I don't think it's possible."

"They had to have been switched when they were tiny," Piper said. "It's the only explanation."

"But then . . . then who am I?" Lily asked.

"And how could we be switched without anyone knowing?" Drew put in.

"Magic," said a dry voice behind them. Piper jumped, spinning around in surprise. There, in the foyer, stood Mr. Elson, Drew's father. And behind him, wearing her usual polite smile, was Mrs. Elson.

"We've come to take our daughter back," Mr. Elson said. He stepped forward and grinned at them, revealing a double row of knifelike teeth. "Come along, Drew."

Piper gaped at him. "I should have known!" she cried. "You're a demon!"

"Demons?" Drew said in a trembling voice. "I was raised by *demons*?"

"None of your lip, young lady," Mr. Elson snapped. "You're coming home right now."

"No, I'm not," Drew retorted. "You're not my real parents. You can't tell me what to do."

Mr. Elson advanced on her, his already large frame growing larger with every step. Soon he was almost eight feet tall. Drew blanched, backing away from him. "How dare you say no to me!" he yelled. "You ungrateful little brat!"

"That's it." Piper raised her hand to explode him. Mrs. Elson opened her mouth and spat, hurling a sticky, spiderweb-like substance through the air. It landed on Piper's hands and contracted, pulling her arms down against her sides and pinning them there.

"Oh, gross," Paige cried, rushing over to help. Piper struggled against the web, but it felt like steel bands encasing her.

"Let's go." Mr. Elson reached for Drew. Juliana stepped in front of her and glared up at him, unafraid.

"You have a lot to answer for," she said coldly. "I want to know how you stole my child. And I want to know where you got Lily from."

He looked her up and down, then turned to his wife. "I told you we shouldn't let her make friends with that mortal," he complained.

"We needed to keep tabs on Juliana, to be

sure she never realized who her daughter really was," his wife replied.

"But our efforts were useless," he said. "She's gone and found her mother."

"I've had to put up with that whining little witch for thirteen years," Mrs. Elson answered. "I will *make* her useful." As she spoke, her bland, pretty face began to widen, turning a grayish-brown mottled color. Her body thickened too, arms growing longer and shoulders broader.

"In her demon form she's as wide as he is tall," Paige murmured, still trying to peel the web off Piper. "I wonder if the other demons make fun of them."

Juliana narrowed her eyes and tried to set the demon woman on fire. There was a brief spark in the air about three inches from her ugly face, then nothing. The demon woman spat at her, but Juliana leaped out of the way in time to avoid the web, setting it on fire instead.

Paige had managed to get one of Piper's arms loose. With her free hand, Piper yanked the web off the rest of her, raised her hands, and exploded the demon woman. At least she tried to. But nothing happened.

"Stupid witch," Mrs. Elson hissed. "We're protected from your kind. Couldn't risk our own witch brat accidentally harming us, now could we?"

Piper thought back to her time in Drew's

bedroom. She hadn't been able to make her powers work there; they must have put some kind of magic-dampening spell around Drew's room. And now they'd put it around themselves, too.

"How do we vanquish them?" Paige asked as Phoebe made her way over to her sisters.

"Anyone got a spell off the top of their heads?" Piper asked.

Phoebe and Paige looked blank. "I wasn't expecting *more* demons today," Phoebe said helplessly.

"We are leaving," Mr. Elson announced, holding out one giant hand. "Come, Drew."

"No way," she replied. "I'm not going with you. You've been lying to me since I was a baby."

Mr. Elson towered over her, using all his bulk to intimidate the small girl. "Peanut butter fluff," he bellowed.

There was a startled silence.

"Okay," Drew said agreeably. She took his hand, and he, Mrs. Elson, and Drew shimmered out of the attic.

Juliana let out a cry of dismay.

"Whoa! What just happened?" Paige asked.

"Why did she go with them?" Lily cried, horrified. "Where did they take her?"

"I don't know. They probably wouldn't go home, since we know where they live." Piper turned to her husband. "What did he say to her? 'Peanut butter fluff'?"

Leo nodded, looking just as confused as she felt.

"What does that mean?" Juliana asked. "I don't get it. Was he offering her peanut butter fluff if she went with them?"

"Seems like it," Piper replied. "But that doesn't make any sense."

Phoebe was already running for the stairs. "I'm going to make a vanquishing potion," she said. "We can't leave Drew in the hands of those demons."

Juliana nodded nervously. "We have to find her," she said. "Now I'm feeling guilty for never calling Social Services on her parents. She was always complaining about them."

"Speaking of which," Paige said, "I think I'm going to head into the office."

"You're going to work?" Piper asked, incredulous. "We have an innocent out there in the hands of very rude web-spitting demons."

"Exactly," Paige replied. "Demons who stole a baby. *Two* babies, probably," she added with a glance at Lily. "I want to see if there are any records on them. I should be able to use the system at work to access police reports from thirteen years ago. Plus, I can see if there are any records of their having done this before."

"Oh. Good idea," Piper said.

"I'm going to check with the Elders," Leo announced. "It seems like the Elsons had Drew surrounded by some kind of magical force field all these years. That's probably why the Elders didn't know who she was," he continued. "But now that they do, they may be able to help us." He gave Piper a quick kiss and orbed away.

Piper glanced around the wrecked attic, trying to ignore the mess. Juliana and Lily both looked exhausted. Piper felt like she could sleep for a week too. Fighting Gortag had taken a lot of stamina. But they had to save Drew before they could rest.

"Let's get to work," she said.

Phoebe stirred the pot of boiling hawthorne leaves for the vanquishing potion as Piper bustled around the kitchen, gathering other ingredients. Juliana was scrying for the demons in the living room, and Lily sat numbly on a stool at the kitchen counter. Phoebe couldn't take her eyes off the poor girl. What must she be going through?

It's hard enough being a thirteen-year-old without magical interference, she thought. When she was Lily's age, she hadn't known about her family's Wiccan heritage. Maybe their mom had been right to keep the truth from them—it seemed too big for a young girl to handle. In one day Lily had gone from expecting to be a witch to learning that she was not only a regular non-Wiccan mortal, but also that she wasn't her mother's daughter. Not to mention losing her best friend to a couple of demons.

"How are you doing, Lily?" she asked gently.

Lily shrugged. "I'm worried about Drew."

"We'll get her back," Phoebe told her. "I promise."

"Will they . . . will they take me away from my mom now?" Lily asked, holding back tears. "Since Drew is her real daughter and I'm not?"

Phoebe's heart broke for the poor kid. "Do you remember what your mom told you before?" she said. "Out in the garden?"

Lily nodded. "She said she'd love me even if I didn't want my powers."

"Right," Phoebe said. "That means she still loves you even though you aren't a witch."

"But I'm not even her daughter," Lily said.

"Oh, yes you are," Juliana told her, coming into the kitchen. She put her arms around Lily and held her tight. "You'll always be my daughter, and I'll always love you."

"You won't let them take me away?"

"No," Juliana said.

"But at some point you may want to find out about your birth parents," Phoebe said. "And that's okay."

"Absolutely," Juliana agreed. "But for now, we're going to get Drew back, and then the three of us will live together."

"I still don't understand why she just went with them," Lily said. "Drew doesn't even like peanut butter fluff."

The answer hit Phoebe like a thunderbolt. "It's a trigger word," she cried. "They knew Drew would do whatever they wanted as long as they said 'peanut butter fluff.'"

"What do you mean?" Piper asked, adding a small rowan twig to the potion.

"It's called conditioning," Phoebe told her. "They did something to Drew to make sure she'd obey them. All they had to do was say the correct phrase, and she would respond however they'd conditioned her to respond."

"They brainwashed her?" Lily asked.

"Sort of," Phoebe replied. "Although I'm sure they did it magically."

"That makes sense," Leo said, orbing in. "The Elders know these demons."

"Well, why didn't they tell us about them before?" Piper asked.

"They didn't know the demons were back," Leo explained. "Apparently they go out of commission for decades at a time."

"You mean they go into hiding?" Juliana asked.

"More like hibernation, or just shutting themselves down," Leo said. "They steal children and use the energy from the children to live. They sort of gorge themselves on the child's life force. And when they're full, they go off and sleep in their lair for twenty or thirty years."

"They're *clan-goids*!" Lily and Juliana said together.

"They're whoosie-whats?" Phoebe asked.

"Clan-goids," Juliana said. "There's a family story about them. You're supposed to put a protective spell around your child until it's one year old. It wards off the baby-snatching imps. We called them imps, but I guess they're demons. I thought it was an old wives' tale."

"It's like Paige said," Phoebe told her. "Your family has an oral history tradition—every single story you learned has some piece of real truth in it."

"I just wish they'd handed down the baby protection spell along with the story," Juliana said. "Then maybe I could've stopped this from happening."

"It's not your fault," Phoebe told her. "It's the demons' fault. They're the bad guys."

"They probably went after Drew because they knew she was a witch," Leo said. "If they could raise her until she got her powers, then force her to use her abilities for evil purposes, there would be a huge amount of negative energy created."

"They figured they could live for years on that," Piper speculated.

"So how do we defeat them?" Phoebe asked.

"I couldn't find them by scrying," Juliana said. "They must still have their magic force field up."

"Oh, I did find out how to get rid of that," Leo said. "It's a pretty simple potion." He handed a slip of paper to Phoebe, and she got to work on the new potion. "But we'll have to find them first," Leo added.

"Can you sense Drew?" Piper asked.

"Probably," he said. "I think I was sensing her all along whenever I tried to sense Lily." His eyes took on a faraway look as he concentrated on Drew. "I think I've got her," he said. "It's distorted, probably by the clan-goids' magic."

"Where is she?" Juliana asked.

"In a store, I think," he said. "I see jewelry. . . . The images I'm getting from her are really strange. She might be in an animal form. She's in a safe or a storeroom. . . ."

"They're probably making her rob the store by sneaking in as a fly or something," Piper said. "Phoebe, how long will this trigger word thing work?"

"I'm not sure," Phoebe replied. "It's not something they teach you much about in psych classes. It isn't ethical to try to brainwash people."

"Can you make a guess?" Piper asked. "If Drew just goes along with their evil plans, it will technically be her own fault. She's still under that forty-eight-hour new witch rule."

"That's true," Leo said. "If she commits evil acts now, it will be like choosing the side of evil. She may get locked into being an evil witch without meaning to."

"But robbing a store wouldn't exactly be evil," Juliana pointed out.

"Well, it isn't exactly *good*," Piper retorted.

"I know, but who gets hurt?" Juliana argued.

"Well, the shopkeeper for one," Leo said. "But in this case, I think Drew would be hurt the most."

"They're going to get her to do things that are wrong," Piper explained. "It doesn't even matter if they're small things. What matters is that once Drew gets used to a pattern of behavior that involves committing crimes or just generally being bad—"

"Then she'll be on the road to becoming evil," Juliana finished. "I get it."

"They've been doing that all her life," Lily put in. "They always told her she was bad, and eventually she started doing bad things. You know, skipping school and lying and stuff."

"So doing even one bad thing now could push her over the edge," Juliana said sadly. "She already thinks of herself as a delinquent. How do we help her?"

"I think the way it works is that they would train her to obey them once they say the trigger word or phrase," Phoebe said, thinking aloud. "Then there would be another word to release her. It's almost as if she's hypnotized—when they say one word, she stops thinking for herself. When they say another word, she starts again. She may not even remember what happens when she's under their control."

"So if they told her to rob a bank, she would?" Lily asked. "Or to kill someone?"

"It's possible," Phoebe said.

"Then we better get to her fast," Juliana said. "Can we orb there?"

"Let's go," Leo said, holding out his hand.

Phoebe pulled a small glass bottle off a shelf and then dipped it into the pot on the stove. "Both potions are ready," she said, corking the bottle.

"Lily, maybe you should stay here," Juliana said.

"No way!" Lily cried, offended. "Drew's my best friend. She's my *sister*. I have to be there for her."

"I would feel the same way," Phoebe said, smiling at her own sister.

"Then everyone grab on," Leo said. They all crowded around him, and he orbed them to the store.

Drew twitched her nose. It smelled strange in here. The room was full of boxes, all neatly stacked on shelves and filled with shiny jewels and other antiques. But her mother only wanted one of them—a large emerald that used to belong to an enemy of hers. She wanted it as a trophy, since she was still alive but her enemy had been vanquished.

Find the emerald, chew through the box, hold it in my mouth until I get back out to Mom and Dad, she thought. Those had been her father's instructions. But the human part of Drew's rat mind couldn't help noticing the flaws in the plan. For one thing, a rat in a store was likely to be noticed. She'd only made it into the storeroom by walking in as a girl and then transforming herself in the bathroom. For another thing, it was hard to read the labels on the boxes with her weak rat eyes. She knew what the box holding the emerald should say, but at her current height, all the words were so big that she could only make out one letter at a time. It was slow going. And finally, she didn't know how long it had been since her mother had seen this emerald, but times seemed to have changed. The boxes in the storeroom weren't made of cardboard. They were all thick metal containers, like safe-deposit boxes. She couldn't chew through those.

If I shapeshift back into my human form, I can do this much faster, she thought. The storeroom was empty. There might be security cameras, though. Trying to puzzle out a plan, Drew sat up on her hind legs and twitched her whiskers. It was hard to think for some reason. She felt as if her brain had been wrapped in a roll of cotton. Maybe being a rat made it difficult to think like a human? But that hadn't been the case before, when she was a squirrel and a mouse. . . .

Something nagged at the edges of Drew's mind. She couldn't remember much about what had happened before her parents brought her to

this antique store. Other witches . . . her friend
Lily . . . Lily's mother . . .

There was a loud noise in the main room of
the store. Instinctively Drew scurried under a
shelf for cover. She would wait until the hub-
bub died down, then she would change herself
back into a girl and steal the emerald for her
mother.

"We need a distraction!" Piper said. She, Leo,
and Phoebe stood surrounding Mr. Elson, while
Juliana and Lily had Mrs. Elson cornered
between an antique rocking chair and a jewelry
case. The demons probably wouldn't dare use
their powers in public. Unfortunately the witches
couldn't use *their* powers either. It was a standoff.
And any minute Drew might steal whatever
she'd come here to steal. She would've made her
choice to join the side of evil. They had to find
her before it was too late.

"Juliana, can you do something?" Piper asked.

Juliana nodded. She glanced around the
shop, crowded with expensive old furniture and
jewelry. Then she narrowed her eyes, and a
sewing dummy in the window burst into flames.
Nice choice, Piper thought. The window was
mostly empty, clearly waiting for a new display
to be put up. There was little chance the fire
would spread to the rest of the store. But they
still didn't have much time.

"Fire!" someone yelled. "Everyone outside!"

Patrons began running for the door, but Piper just turned back to Mr. Elson. "Where's Drew?" she demanded.

"Stealing a jewel that we like," he said calmly. "It's only the first step. She'll do whatever I tell her to do."

"Lily, go check the back rooms for Drew," Piper cried. "Hurry!" Lily took off through the now-empty store. Piper heard fire engine sirens in the distance. She threw the first potion down at Mr. Elson's feet. He sniffed at it, unconcerned.

"What's the release word?" Phoebe demanded. "How do we snap Drew out of this brain-washing?"

Mr. Elson chuckled. "Why would I tell you that?" he asked.

Piper turned and exploded his wife. "You're next," she said. "Unless you tell us."

Mr. Elson bellowed in outrage.

"Oh yeah, that potion broke down your force field," Piper told him. "Now tell us how to release Drew."

Mr. Elson grew to his full demon height almost instantly. "You will pay for that, witch!" he yelled. He raised his giant fist to strike.

"Drew!" Lily called. "Drew, it's me! Where are you?" She paused and looked around the tiny storeroom. This was the third room she'd tried. Drew could be anywhere. She might be a fly on the wall for all Lily knew.

"Drew, don't steal anything!" she called.

Suddenly she felt something soft brush against her ankle. Lily looked down to see a white rat rubbing against her leg. "Drew," she said softly. She bent to look in the rat's eyes. "Can you come back to normal?"

The rat ran into the middle of the room and stood on its hind legs, nose in the air. Then the rat grew taller, while at the same time the white hair vanished. In a few seconds Drew stood before her, looking a little confused.

"We have to get out of here," Lily said, grabbing her friend's hand.

Drew pulled away. "I have to find an emerald first," she said, turning to look at the labels on some metal boxes.

"No, you can't!" Lily cried. "You would be stealing, and that means you'd be choosing to be evil."

"My parents told me to," Drew said emotionlessly.

"They're not your parents, they're demons!" Lily argued. "You don't have to listen to them. They brainwashed you."

Drew pulled a box off the shelf. "Here it is," she said. She started to open the box.

Piper froze Mr. Elson just before his fist made contact with her face. She quickly moved away from him. The sirens were getting louder—people would be here any second.

"What will happen if we vanquish both of them without learning the release word?" she asked Phoebe.

"I'm not sure," her sister replied. "The effects of the trigger word could vanish, leaving Drew totally back in control of herself."

"That would be good," Piper said.

"Or else the effects could last forever, or until we stumble on the release word."

"That would be bad," Piper said. But did they really have a choice?

"Drew, no!" Lily's voice yelled in one of the back rooms. The squeal of brakes announced that a fire truck had just pulled up outside. They were out of time. Piper pulled the vial containing the vanquishing potion out of her pocket and threw it at Mr. Elson. He vanished in a puff of smoke just as the first firefighter entered the shop.

"Hey!" he yelled, jogging over to them as his partner doused the blazing dress dummy with a fire extinguisher. "You were supposed to evacuate. What are you doing in here?"

"Looking for my daughter," Juliana piped up. "She went in the back to find a bathroom, and we didn't want to leave her in here with the place on fire."

As if to prove her words, Lily appeared from the back, Drew behind her. But which Drew would it be—a good witch or an evil one?

"You folks better get outside now," the firefighter said. "There's still a lot of smoke in here."

"Yes, sir," Phoebe said, leading the way out.

On the sidewalk they all turned to Drew. Piper studied the girl's face. "What happened?" she asked.

"They told me to steal an emerald that my mother wanted," Drew said. She smiled at Juliana. "I mean, my *fake* mother. But Lily stopped me."

"How?" Phoebe asked Lily.

"I just told her she had to choose between stealing the emerald and being my friend," Lily said proudly. "And she chose. She didn't even need a stupid release word. She just needed me!"

"That's what sisters are for," Drew said. She held up her hand and Lily slapped her a high five.

Grinning, Piper turned to Phoebe. "Oh, why not?" Phoebe said, holding up her hand. And Piper gave her own sister a triumphant high five too.

A month later Phoebe was just finishing up her column when Paige burst through the front door. "Good news!" she called.

Piper looked up from the pasta sauce she was making. "What?" she asked.

"I just got the final paperwork transferring custody of Drew to Juliana," Paige told them. "The blood test proved that Juliana is Drew's birth mother, and that's all the judge needed."

"That's great," Phoebe said. "But what about

the inquiry into how the babies got switched?"

"It's ongoing," Paige replied. "But they'll never find the hospital to be at fault, because Lily was born in a totally different hospital. I think they'll just keep looking for the baby snatcher who did it, but they'll never find anyone."

"Too bad they don't know to look for a clangoid," Piper joked.

"But there's some sad news too," Paige added. "I found Lily's birth mother—well, I found her obituary, anyway."

"Oh, no." Phoebe was filled with sadness. "When did she die?"

"Six years ago," Paige said. "She had cancer."

"It's a good thing Lily has such a loving mother in Juliana," Piper said.

"Yeah. Also, her birth father is still alive," Paige added. "Juliana already contacted him. The demons had brainwashed him into forgetting Lily ever existed. But once we vanquished them, it all came back. He'll be thrilled to meet her."

Phoebe sighed happily. "So we've set up another witch family for a happy life," she said. "Makes ya feel good, doesn't it?"

"It makes me appreciate our own ancestors for writing things down," Paige joked.

"Yeah, but it's good to remember how important family history is," Piper said. "Because without family, where would we be?"

Phoebe picked up her coffee mug and offered

a toast. "To witch families everywhere," she said. "But most of all, to my favorite witch family, right here at home."

And as the Charmed Ones clinked their cups together they could feel all the other Halliwell witches who had lived in that house silently toasting with them.

About the Author

Laura J. Burns is best known for writing the TV show *Roswell*, and she's written numerous books for the Buffy, Charmed, Roswell, and Everwood book series. She lives in Los Angeles, California.

THE BOOK
OF THREE

The first ever authorised Charmed Companion!

Everything you ever wanted to know about The Charmed Ones – Piper, Paige and Phoebe and their world of Wicca. This complete guide features a series overview, character profiles and interviews with the crew and cast. This Charmed Companion also includes The Beginners Book of Wicca – a discussion of the basic tenets of Wicca and how they relate to the show; The Book of Shadows – a compilation of the spells used on each show; and The Book of Evil – a complete who's who of the various demons that appear in the hit show. Complete with black and white photographs throughout and a 16 page full colour photo insert, *The Book of Three* is a must for every Charmed fan!

A TALE OF
TWO PIPERS

Coming soon!

ISBN: 0689872720   £4.99

. . . A GIRL BORN
WITHOUT THE FEAR GENE

FEARLESS™

A SERIES BY
FRANCINE PASCAL

PUBLISHED BY POCKET BOOKS

All Pocket books are available by post from:

Simon & Schuster Cash Sales.
PO Box 29
Douglas, Isle of Man
IM99 1BQ

Credit cards accepted.

Please telephone 01624 836000
fax 01624 670923,
Internet http://www.bookpost.co.uk
or email: bookshop@enterprise.net
for details